Max Frisch (1911-1991) was born in Zurich, Switzerland before the First World War and was a soldier in the Second. In the interwar years, he traveled throughout Eastern and central Europe as a journalist. After serving as a gunner on the Austrian and Italian borders, he followed in his father's footsteps and became an architect. These experiences helped forge the moral consciousness and the concern for human freedom that mark his writing. The author of *I'm Not Stiller, Homo Faber, Montauk,* and *Gantenbein*, Frisch was one of Europe's most important postwar writers.

T0273312

Other books by Max Frisch

Man in the Holocene
Max Frisch

A STORY

Translated from German by Geoffrey Skelton

DALKEY ARCHIVE PRESS
Champaign • London

Library of Congress Cataloging-in-Publication Data

Frisch, Max, 1911-1991.
  [Mensch erscheint im Holozän. English]
  Man in the holocene / Max Frisch ; translation by Geoffrey Skelton. -- 1st Dalkey
Archive ed.
        p. cm.
  ISBN-13: 978-1-56478-466-7 (alk. paper)
  ISBN-10: 1-56478-466-5 (alk. paper)
  I. Skelton, Geoffrey. II. Title.
  PT2611.R814M4413 2007
  843 ' .914--dc22

                                          2006036442

This publication is partially supported by the National Endowment for the Arts, a federal agen~
the Illinois Arts Council, a state agency, and the University of Illinois, Urbana-Champaign.

www.dalkeyarchive.com

FOR MARIANNE

Man in the Holocene

It should be possible to build a pagoda of crispbread, to think of nothing, to hear no thunder, no rain, no splashing from the gutter, no gurgling around the house. Perhaps no pagoda will emerge, but the night will pass.

Somewhere a tapping on metal.

It is always with the fourth floor that the wobbling begins; a trembling hand as the next piece of crispbread is put in place, a cough when the gable is already standing, and the whole thing lies in ruins—

Geiser has time to spare.

The news in the village is conflicting; some people say there has been no landslide at all, others that an old supporting wall has collapsed, and there is no way of diverting the highway at that spot. The woman in the post office, who ought to know, merely confirms that the mail bus is not running, but she stands behind the little counter in her usual care-laden fashion, keeping usual office hours, selling stamps, and even accepting parcels, which she places unhurriedly on the scales and then franks. It is taken for granted that state and canton are doing everything in their power to get the highway back in order. If necessary, helicopters can be brought in, unless there is fog. Nobody in the village thinks that the day, or perhaps the night, will come when the whole mountain could begin to slide, burying the village for all time.

Somewhere a tapping on metal.

It is midnight, but still no pagoda.

It started on the Thursday of the previous week, when it was still possible to sit out in the open; the weather was sultry, as always before a thunderstorm, the gnats biting through one's socks; no summer lightning, it just felt uncomfortable. Not a bird in the grounds. His guests, a youngish couple on their way to Italy, suddenly decided to leave, though they could have spent the night in his house. It was not actually cloudy—just a yellowish haze, such as one sees in the Arabian desert before a sandstorm; no wind. Faces also looking yellowish. His guests did not even empty their glasses, they were suddenly in such a hurry to be off, though there were no sounds of thunder. Not a drop of rain, either. But on the following morning it was drumming on the windowpanes, hissing through the leaves of the chestnut tree.

Since then, not a night without thunderstorms and cloudbursts.

From time to time the power is cut, something one is used to in this valley; hardly has there been time to find a candle, and then at last some matches, when the power is restored, lights in the house, though the thunder continues.

4

———

It is not so much the bad weather—

The twelve-volume encyclopedia DER GROSSE BROCK-
HAUS explains what causes lightning and distinguishes
streak lightning, ball lightning, bead lightning, etc., but
there is little to be learned about thunder; yet in the course
of a single night, unable to sleep, one can distinguish at
least nine types of thunder:

1.
The simple thunder crack.

2.
Stuttering or tottering thunder: this usually comes after a
lengthy silence, spreads across the whole valley, and can
go on for minutes on end.

3.
Echo thunder: shrill as a hammer striking on loose metal
and setting up a whirring, fluttering echo which is louder
than the peal itself.

4.
Roll or bump thunder: relatively unfrightening, for it is
reminiscent of rolling barrels bumping against one another.

5.
Drum thunder.

6.
Hissing or gravel thunder: this begins with a hiss, like a
truck tipping a load of wet gravel, and ends with a thud.

7.

Bowling-pin thunder: like a bowling pin that, struck by the rolling ball, cannons into the other pins and knocks them all down; this causes a confused echo throughout the valley.

8.

Hesitant or tittering thunder (no flash of lightning through the windows): this indicates that the storm is retreating over the mountains.

9.

Blast thunder (immediately following a flash of lightning through the windows): this is not like two hard masses colliding; on the contrary, it is like a single huge mass being blasted apart and falling to either side, breaking into countless pieces; in its wake, rain comes pouring down.

At intervals the power goes off again.

What would be bad would be losing one's memory—

An example of something Geiser has not forgotten: the Pythagorean theorem. For that he does not need to drag out the encyclopedia. On the other hand, he cannot remember how to draw the golden section (A is to B as A + B to A; that he does still know) with compasses and set square. He knew once, of course—

No knowledge without memory.

Today is Tuesday.

Still no horns sounding in the valley.

Field glasses are no use at all in times like these, one screws them this way and that without being able to find any sharp outline to bring into focus; all they do is make the mist thicker. What can be seen with the naked eye: the gutter on the roof, the nearest pine tree in the grounds, two wires disappearing into the mist, raindrops gliding slowly down the wires. If one takes an umbrella and trudges through the grounds on a tour of inspection despite wet and mist, one can no longer see one's own house after only a hundred paces, just brambles in mist, rivulets, bracken in mist. A little wall in the lower garden (dry-stone) has collapsed: debris among the lettuces, lumps of clay under the tomatoes. Perhaps that happened days ago.

Still, one can get tomatoes in cans.

Lavender flowering in the mist: scentless, as in a color film. One wonders what bees do in a summer like this.

There are provisions enough in the house:

three eggs
bouillon cubes
tea
vinegar and olive oil
flour
onions
a jar of pickled gherkins
Parmesan cheese
sardines, one can

7

spices of all kinds
crispbread, five packages
garlic
raspberry syrup for the grandchildren
anchovies
bay leaves
semolina
salted almonds
spaghetti, one package
olives
Ovomaltine
one lemon
meat in the icebox

Later in the day there is more thunder; and shortly afterward, hail. The white stones, some of them the size of
hazelnuts, dance on the granite table; in a few minutes
the lawn is a white sheet, all Geiser can do is stand at the
window and watch the vine being torn to shreds, the roses,
too—

There is nothing to do but read.

(Novels are no use at all on days like these, they deal with
people and their relationships, with themselves and others,
fathers and mothers and daughters or sons, lovers, etc.,
with individual souls, usually unhappy ones, with society,
etc., as if the place for these things were assured, the earth
for all time earth, the sea level fixed for all time.)

No horns sounding in the valley.

Obviously the highway is still blocked.

When, occasionally, the rain eases up—it does not stop entirely, but becomes lighter, so that one no longer hears it on the roof, rain just seen as a noiseless shading over the darkness of the nearest pine tree—the silence is still not complete; on the contrary, one then begins to hear the rushing of water down in the valley; there must be streams everywhere, streams that normally do not exist. A constant rushing sound throughout the valley.

> **The Creation of the World**
> (Job 38; Ps. 33:6–9; Ps. 104; Prov. 8:22–31)
>
> In the beginning God created the heaven and the earth.
> 2 And the earth was without form, and void; and darkness was upon the face of the deep. And the Spirit of God moved upon the face of the waters.

Geiser wonders whether there would still be a God if there were no longer a human brain, which cannot accept the idea of a creation without a creator.

Today is Wednesday.

(Or Thursday?)

One can hardly call it a library that Geiser has at his disposal during these days in which gardening is impossible;

Elsbeth read novels mainly, the classics and others, Geiser himself preferring factual books (BRIGHTER THAN A THOUSAND SUNS); the diary of Captain Scott, who froze to death at the South Pole—Geiser has read this several times, but it is a very long while since he last read the Bible. Besides the twelve-volume encyclopedia there are: gardening books, a book on snakes, a history of the canton of Ticino, the Swiss encyclopedia, as well as picture books for the grandchildren (THE WORLD WE LIVE IN), the Duden dictionary of foreign words, and a book about Iceland, which Geiser once visited thirty years ago, as well as maps and rambling guides that provide information about the geology, climate, history, etc., of the district.

CHAPTER I
Ticino in Prehistoric Times
The First Inhabitants

In the far-distant epochs of geological antiquity, the present canton of Ticino, like all else, lay for long periods submerged beneath the deep sea extending between two age-old continents to the north and the south. Massive layers of sedimentary rock were formed in that ocean, and these piled up on the crystal rocks of the ocean bed.

As sections of the earth's crust emerged above sea level, the natural forces of weathering and erosion at once began their work of shaping and displacing. Frost and wind produced ridges and peaks on the raised masses of rock, while water and glaciers ate into the furrows and carved out the first valleys. This was no continuous process: it was spread over various periods, widely separated in time. This we can discern without difficulty from the many terraces running parallel to one another along the valley slopes, each of which must once have formed the valley bed.

In the main valleys the force of the glaciers was far greater than in the subsidiary valleys, and the rivers are in consequence deeper than their tributaries. For this reason the beds of the subsidiary valleys have remained higher than those of the main valleys, and the tributaries flow over sheer ledges into the main rivers. This explains the many waterfalls, which give the Ticino valley its wild and romantic appearance.

On the other hand, we know more about the people who came to live in this district during the *Iron Age* (c.800–58 B.C.). The discovery of graves from the earliest Ice Age,[4] the so-called Ligurian period, on the one hand; and place and field names[5] on the other, show that the Ticino district at that time was inhabited by the *Ligures*. History tells us that in earliest antiquity the Ligures made settlements, not only in present-day Liguria, but also in the valleys of the Western Alps, to which the territory of present-day Ticino belongs.

Finally, mention must be made of the many rockfalls that have occurred since the retreat of the glaciers, for they played no little part in giving many districts in the canton of Ticino the appearance they have today.

According to legend, one of Hercules's tasks was to lead a tribe of people across the Alps into Spain and then into Africa. On the march through the deep snow of the Alpine passes, a rear guard was left behind. Many soldiers froze to death, and the survivors were unable to re-establish contact with the main column, which had gone on ahead. They made no further attempt to advance, but settled down in Alpine lands. The word "Lepontine" means "those who stayed behind." That these Lepontines, whose name has in fact been applied in the course of time to a large number of other tribes, did populate both slopes of the Gotthard—this we know from completely reliable sources, such as the Roman naturalist Pliny the Elder (A.D. 23–79) and Julius Caesar (100–44 B.C.).

It is not true, incidentally, that no horns are sounding in the valley; it is just that the mail bus is not running, one misses its three-note horn, and the noisy trucks that usually carry the slabs and blocks of granite down into the valley are not working; but above the spot where the highway has been cut there are still motorcycles.

One has just sounded its horn now.

The encyclopedia explains how to draw the golden section with compasses and set square, and even if there are no compasses in the house, Geiser knows what he has to do: a thumbtack, a piece of thread fixed to the thumbtack, and a pencil fixed to the other end of the thread replace the compasses after a fashion. At the moment Geiser has no use for a golden section, but knowledge is reassuring.

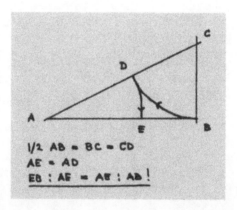

1/2 AB = BC = CD
AE = AD
EB : AE = AE : AB !

The little landslide in the garden (debris among the lettuces) has not grown any bigger during the night. And as far as Geiser can see in the morning twilight, there have been no new landslides, at least not in his grounds. The grayish clay beneath the tomatoes, which are still green, sticks to the spade in heavy lumps. And when Geiser tries without a spade, going down on his knees and clearing the debris around the lettuces with his hands, the lettuces are in any case spoiled, and the time is not right to set about repairing the little wall. That will take days. Within an hour one is wet right through, despite raincoat and hat.

No sounds of a helicopter.

The collapse of a little dry-stone wall, built with his own hands by a pensioner who has spent his life doing other things, does not mean that the whole slope is beginning to slide. Presumably there are rivulets here and there and lumps of clay, these are usual in persistent rain. Presumably on the steep slopes a tree has toppled over here and there, an old pine or a rotting chestnut; its trunk will then be lying with its smashed crown pointing down the slope, the black roots spread out in the air and the rock exposed, gneiss or schist, elsewhere nagelfluh.

During the night of September 30, 1512 (at the very time the Duke of Milan was negotiating with the Swiss for the surrender of Lugano and Locarno), the peak of Monte Crenone overhanging Biasca exploded without warning on the side overlooking the Pontirone valley; the ensuing rock-falls buried a great many houses with all their occupants, while from the opposite slopes of the mountain huge masses of earth slid down and engulfed the village of Campo Bargigno in Val Calanca.

It was not until three centuries later that the Ticino bridge destroyed in that catastrophe was rebuilt (1812–1815). At one corner of the "büzza"* near Biasca one comes upon the surprising sight of a church steeple poking out through the

13

rocks and gorse bushes: it is the church tower of Loderio. This curious ruin recalls another great disaster, one vivid to many people still living: the great floods of 1868, which buried the church of Loderio, destroyed all bridges in the Blenio valley, and brought terror and death to Malvaglia, Semione, Dongio, and especially to Corzoneso. During the night of September 27 a raging flood swept without warning over Cumiasca, in the district of Corzoneso, destroying the village completely and claiming eighteen human lives. The compassion of all Europe was stirred as it listened aghast to reports of the terrible distress caused by these floods in Blenio, in Levantina, in Verzasca, and in Vallemaggia. Aid funds totaling two million francs were collected. Pope Pius contributed several thousand lire, Emperor Napoleon twenty thousand francs, the Grand Duke of Baden ten thousand.

On March 23, 1851, after snow had been falling continuously for three days, several huge avalanches broke loose from the summits of the surrounding mountains and, following quite unusual courses, swept down with tremendous force on the unfortunate village, burying nine homesteads. Twenty-three human beings and over three hundred head of cattle perished. In connection with this event Lavizzari has written: "The disastrous masses of snow that had deprived them of their herds, their homes, and their families were hardly melted away before the survivors took heart again and rebuilt their huts in Cozzera, just as the people whose homes had been destroyed by the glowing ashes of Vesuvius hardly waited for the monster to close its flaming jaws before starting immediately to think of rebuilding their houses on the hot lava."

Last night there were stars to be seen, though not many, and even, for minutes on end, the moon between racing clouds, veils of whitish mist in the lower valley, the wet cliffs above glittering in places like aluminum foil, and the moon above the black woods looked more arid than ever—

Today it is gurgling again.

But at least it is not snowing.

His rucksack is lying in the hallway, a leather rucksack that Geiser bought on his visit to Iceland, waterproof, and Geiser has thought of everything: passport, bandages, flashlight, a change of underclothing, Ovomaltine, a change of socks, iodine, a small book of travelers' checks, aspirin, Miroton (for cardiac insufficiency), as well as a compass and a magnifying glass for deciphering the map, CARTA NAZIONALE DELLA SVIZZERA 1:25,000, FOGLIO 1312 and 1311, though Geiser is well aware that to attempt an escape over the mountains (into Italy) would be madness. Something that maybe a young man might venture. Even the old mule track down into the valley, which Geiser once followed years ago, would probably be blocked now by streams full of debris, a perilous path—he does not need anyone to tell him that.

Today is Wednesday.

A summer guest from Germany, a professor of astronomy, knows a lot about the sun and, if asked, is not unwilling to talk about it, even to a layman. Afterward one clears the cups away, grateful for the short visit. Geiser understood more or less what is meant by prominences, which incidentally have nothing to do with the weather on earth, and the solar investigator's wife brought along a bowl of soup, minestrone, to be warmed up. At any rate, one knows afterward that one is not crazy: other people have also noticed that it keeps on raining.

> 17 And the flood was forty days upon the earth; and the waters increased, and bare up the ark, and it was lift up above the earth.
> 18 And the waters prevailed, and were increased greatly upon the earth; and the ark went upon the face of the waters.
> 19 And the waters prevailed exceedingly upon the earth; and all the high hills, that were under the whole heaven, were covered.
> 20 Fifteen cubits upward did the waters prevail; and the mountains were covered.
> 21 And all flesh died that moved upon the earth, both of fowl, and of cattle, and of beast, and of every creeping thing that creepeth upon the earth, and every man;
> 22 All in whose nostrils was the breath of life, of all that was in the dry land, died.
> 23 And every living substance was destroyed which was upon the face of the ground, both man, and cattle, and the creeping things, and the fowl of the heaven; and they were destroyed from the earth: and Noah only remained alive, and they that were with him in the ark.
> 24 And the waters prevailed upon the earth an hundred and fifty days.

Geiser does not believe in the Flood.

The Zurich parson H. R. Schinz also made some interesting observations during the period September 1770 to September

Until a short while ago, June, it was cloudless, the grass
dry and yellowish; at six in the morning, when Geiser
attempted again to attack the grass with a scythe, the sun
itself was not yet visible, just its rays on the peaks and
ridges of the mountains, the valley still in a blue shadow;
shortly after seven o'clock, there was a flash on the scythe,
and suddenly it was hot, a day of biting flies, lizards, butterflies, summer as usual, summer lightning in the evening, no rain, or just a few drops, the following morning
also blue and hot, the white cumulus clouds dry as cotton
wool. For weeks the use of a garden hose was forbidden,
the soil gray and cracked. The little brook below the church
was without water, a dry stone bed.

Geiser knew at one time what caused tides, just as he knew
about volcanoes, mountain ranges, etc. But when did the
first mammals emerge? Instead of this, one knows how
many liters of heating oil the tank contains, the time of the
first and last mail bus—that is, when the highway is not
blocked. When did man first emerge, and why? Triassic,
Jurassic, Cretaceous, etc., but no idea how many millions
of years the various eras lasted.

Among the living creatures of the Triassic period the
ammonites and the belemnites, amphibians, and especially reptiles attained great variety and widespread
distribution, including very large forms, such as the
long-extinct dinosaurs. There were also small types
of mammals (see Triassic System) and birds (see
Jurassic System). From the Jurassic onward there
was a visible division into climatic zones. Plant life,
showing a more marked development than animal
life, was in the Late Permian Era already showing
many Mesozoic characteristics. In the Cretaceous
(see Cretaceous System) it was enriched by deciduous trees, which made their appearance from the
very first in huge numbers. Today's mainlands began
to assume shape in the Late Cretaceous, and in
the Mesozoic geosynclines the mountains of the Alps

18

were already beginning to form, reaching their full development in the Early Cainozoic (Neolithic; *see* Cainozoic System). In the Tertiary (*see* Tertiary Era) mammalia developed in great variety, while many of the reptile groups, ammonites, etc., disappeared. Later in the Tertiary, conditions, including the climatic, came closer to those prevailing today, but the Quaternary (*see* Ice Age) has left its imprint on many parts of the earth's surface. According to present views, man first made his appearance in the Pleistocene (*see* Old Stone Age); the geological present is termed the Holocene (*q.v.*).

It is not enough for Geiser to draw a line with his ball-point pen against passages in this book or that worth remembering; within an hour his memory of them has become hazy; names and dates in particular refuse to stick; the things he does not wish to forget Geiser must write down in his own hand on pieces of paper, which he must then affix to the wall. There are thumbtacks enough in the house.

CAMBRIAN	100,000,000 YEARS
SILURIAN	70,000,000
DEVONIAN	80,000,000
CARBONIFEROUS	75,000,000
PERMIAN	75,000,000
TRIASSIC	80,000,000
JURASSIC	70,000,000
CRETACEOUS	20,000,000
TERTIARY	60,000,000
QUATERNARY	1,000,000

19

Two of the letters Geiser has written since Sunday are already out of date, since the news of a landslide turned out to be incorrect, and the third letter, to his daughter in Basel, will sound absurd if mail deliveries are restored tomorrow or the day after; there are sentences in it that sound like Captain Scott in his tent.

And all it is doing is raining.

One can watch television, TELEVISIONE SVIZZERA ITALIANA, though the reception is bad; at the moment tennis is being played in London, the shadows of the players can be seen clearly on the grass, then it suddenly flickers, and when Geiser turns the knobs, the picture suddenly slides off the screen; the sound is still there, overloud, but the picture slips slowly or swiftly upward or downward, and in the end there is nothing but a tangle of black and white stripes.

In London the sun is shining.

Actually nothing much can happen, even if it keeps on raining for weeks or months; the village lies on a slope, the water is running off, one can hear it gurgling around the house.

At least no mist today—

The valley looks unharmed.

The hot plate is not heating up—

A lake, the color of brown clay, gradually filling the valley, a lake without a name, its water level rising day by day and also during the nights, joining up with the rising lakes in the other valleys until the Alps become an archipelago, a group of rocky islands with glaciers overhanging the sea— impossible to imagine that.

In London the sun is shining.

Actually Geiser is not feeling hungry, it does not matter if the soup, the minestrone that the solar investigator's wife brought along, stays cold—

Probably the whole village is without electricity.

The icebox has not yet started to smell bad, but the butter is soft and runny; obviously the power has been off for some time. The cheese is sweating. Though not really hungry, he eats the last egg, raw—though with some revulsion, since it is not chilled.

The fuses are all in order.

Water in the cellar is not unusual when it has been raining a long time; the gravel floor gets damp because the water seeps up from the slopes.

Also the boiler is not working.

Plenty of wood in the house.

When the highway is not blocked by bad weather one can reach Basel in five hours, Milan in three, the nearest drugstore in half an hour—

One is not at the end of the world!

(—as Elsbeth often used to say.)

Luckily there is not very much in the deepfreeze, which is not working: three cutlets, meat for stuffings, a chop, packages of spinach, a meat loaf for unexpected guests, raspberries in packages, two trout, five sausages. Greenish and reddish drops are exuding from the packages; the meat, usually hard as iron, is flabby, and the trout are repulsive to the touch, the sausages soft as slugs. Geiser knows that foods once thawed out must not be refrozen, so there is no need to waste time in thought—they must be put in a bag and given away in the village, and the sooner the better.

Unfortunately the rain is streaming down again.

The villagers are also without electricity, but confident that it cannot last very much longer, that any minute, as it were, the electricity must come on again—

The church clock has also stopped.

Not even old Ettore, the laborer who has been working all his life on supporting walls, public and otherwise, seriously believes that the whole mountain could ever begin to slide; he just grins through his stubbly white beard. To his face they are friendly, and they thank him for the meat, but basically they consider everybody not born in the valley to be either rich or a bit crazy.

Il Professore di Basilea

That is what they call Geiser, because outside his house he always wears a tie; in fact, they know very well that he is not a professor, and what he once was can be seen on his tax return.

Che tempo, che tempo!

That is all they can think of to say.

When the sun is shining on the granite roofs, when the gutters are not overflowing, when the old walls are not wet, when there are no puddles, when it is not dripping and gurgling everywhere, when the sunflowers are not snapped in the middle, when the church tower rises into a blue sky, when the only splashing comes from the fountain, when one is not picking one's way through rivulets, when the surrounding mountains are not gray, then it is a picturesque village.

Today not a dog barking.

It is not until Geiser gets back to his house with the empty bag, places his dripping umbrella in the entrance hall, takes off his wet shoes, that it occurs to him he could have roasted the meat over the open fire himself, at least the meat loaf, which could also be eaten cold.

One is becoming stupid—!

Even in normal circumstances there are not many lights to be seen during the night, two street lamps (five in the winter, when there are no leaves to hide them) and a few living-room lights in the village, in fine weather one faint light from a lonely farm on the slope opposite; now not a single light throughout the valley.

AT THE END OF THE ICE AGE THE LEVEL
OF THE SEA WAS AT LEAST 100 METERS
LOWER THAN TODAY.

ALWAYS BE PREPARED.

SPEED OF LIGHTNING: 100,000 KILO-
METERS PER SECOND. INTENSITY OF
CURRENT: 20 TO 180,000 AMPERES

CHANGING OF HUMAN BEINGS INTO
ANIMALS, TREES, STONE, ETC.
SEE: METAMORPHOSIS / MYTH.

STONE AGE: 6000 - 4000 B.C.
NEOLITHIC AGE: TO 1800 B.C.

More kinds of thunder:

10.
Groaning or lath thunder: a short, high-pitched crack, as if one were snapping a lath, then a groan, short or prolonged; as a rule, lath thunder is the first to be heard in an approaching storm.

11.
Chatter thunder.

12.
Cushion thunder: this sounds exactly like a housewife beating a cushion with flat hands.

13.
Skid thunder: this leads one to expect either bump or drum thunder, but before the windows begin to rattle, the noise slips over to the other side of the valley, where it coughs itself out, as it were.

14.
Crackle thunder.

15.
Screech or bottle thunder, often more frightening than blast thunder, though it does not make the windows rattle; this belongs to the unexpected thunders: one has seen no lightning flash, yet suddenly there is a shrill, splintering noise, like a case of empty bottles falling down steps.

16.
Whispering thunder,
etc.

Geiser has not yet reached the point of talking to the cat when she rubs herself against his trouser legs. She has already had the last sardines, and the remains of the milk from a can, too; not even this was to her liking, and now she sits crouched in the middle of the room with narrowed eyes, waiting. Obviously she has found nothing in the grounds, no birds, not even lizards. Anchovies she finds too salty. When Geiser lifts her by the scruff of the neck (which does not hurt cats) and puts her in the cellar, where she will perhaps think of looking for mice, she yowls behind the door until Geiser lets her out again. Immediately she starts rubbing against his trouser legs. She just cannot understand that there is no more meat to be had.

The television has stopped working, too, of course.

No idea what is happening in the world.

The last news reports Geiser heard were bad, as usual, ranging from assassinations to unemployment statistics; here and there some government minister resigning, but there is no real reason to suppose that today's news would have been any better; all the same, one feels easier in one's mind when one knows from day to day that life is still going on.

Impossible to work in the garden.

One cannot spend the whole day reading.

The church bell, which chimes at seven in the morning

26

and six in the evening, can be worked by hand, and old Felice is taking care of that as usual; the older he gets, the shorter the chimes—

On the other hand, the clock has stopped striking the hours.

There is nothing to do but read.

Geiser is not in fact expecting a visitor, but somebody could have come to the front door. The bell does not work, of course, without electricity, and so it seems advisable to pin a piece of paper to the door, better still a piece of stiff cardboard:

Sono in casa!

Or perhaps it should be:

Sono a casa.

(Elsbeth would have known.)

Please knock!

I am at home.

Or just factual:

Campanello non funziona.

So now that is done.

And it is still only morning—

Geiser is not usually one of those people who become bored without a business to manage, when the telephone is not ringing all day; there is always something to do or to think about when one lives alone.

At times the encyclopedia offers precious little information.

> The best way to avoid being struck by **lightning** is to remain inside a house fitted with a lightning conductor (*q.v.*). In the open air it is advisable to keep away from trees (of all kinds), fences, or enclosures made of metal. Protection against the indirect effects of lightning through current transmitted via the soil (dangerous up to 40 meters away) is best afforded by a metal net or pieces of metal laid on or under the soil.

There is no fear of a food shortage, though the little grocery store in the village does not have much in stock: salt, baking powder, onions, lemonade, laundry powder, tea, slug pellets, etc.; the butter is all gone, as are the eggs, and no milk even in cans. Obviously people have already started hoarding. Luckily there are still matches to be had —one box per customer! The little store has never stocked meat, except for smoked bacon, and that is all gone. Canned meat, for which Geiser does not usually care, is also gone. The cats in this district are seldom eaten.

CHE TEMPO, CHE TEMPO.

The little carpentry shop below the village is still open, the wet sawdust in front of the workshop dark in color, like tea leaves; not much ever goes on there, the saw is not heard every day.

At the moment the rain has almost stopped.

Here and there on the asphalt lumps of clay, rivulets, but no boulders. A yellow snowplow is standing where it always stands in summer. It is a comfort to Geiser to see no cracks in the asphalt. Somewhere along his way a Dutch family in blue oilskins, their faces pale, but cheerful. Not a word of greeting. They have a summer house here, and for four weeks of the year a Dutch flag is hoisted, even when it is raining. Their dog is wearing a blue oilskin, too. Otherwise there is no one out of doors. A construction site; no work in progress, since the workers from Novara have not arrived; planks floating in the cellar; sacks of cement lying in a puddle; the tarpaulin that was supposed to protect them from the rain has been blown away.

Geiser has his umbrella.

Unfortunately he has forgotten the field glasses.

Once before, in 1970, a piece of the highway below the village vanished in a landslide; on the following morning the iron railings were hanging twisted over the ravine; all through the summer the traffic was held up by repair work, but it was not blocked entirely. Landslides like that have always occurred in this district—

Somewhere along his way, three drenched sheep.

There is no point in asking why Geiser, a citizen of Basel, settled in this valley; he just did.

People can grow old anywhere.

Now and again Geiser stops: the gray sound of rushing waters from the ravine—but the iron railings are still there. When one can walk without an umbrella, when there are not puddles everywhere, when drops are not falling from every fir tree, and when the woods on the opposite slope are not black and the mountains wrapped in cloud, when one can work in the garden, when there are butterflies, when one hears bees and in the night a little owl, when one can stand beside the stream with a fishing rod and is in good health, consequently content, though hooking nothing all day, and when the highway is not blocked, allowing one to leave the valley thrice daily, then it is a picturesque valley—otherwise, German and Dutch people would not come here summer after summer.

The neighboring village is also undamaged.

Puddles here, too—

No dogs in the street—

The post office is open, but Geiser has no letters to send, and the man behind the counter has nothing new to tell, though he lives in hope, he says with a laugh.

RISTORANTE DELLA POSTA:

The red tables in front of it are gleaming wet; a truck that is unable to leave the valley is also gleaming and dripping, standing there for a week loaded with empty bottles:

BIRRA BELLINZONA

The church clock here has also stopped.

The store in which Geiser had hoped to buy matches is closed, the doorbell not working, but matches can be bought in the tavern; no need to sit down to swallow a quick schnapps and then, while paying, to ask casually what day it is.

Why is the landlord so friendly?

So it is Saturday—

That is all Geiser wished to know.

It is a gloomy tavern when one cannot sit outside, and what the few people at the tables are saying is nothing new. A bad year for wine; even for mushrooms the summer has been too wet. Nobody is reckoning on another Flood. The local youngsters, prevented from driving to work in the valley, are obviously set to spend all day working the noisy soccer machine. A second schnapps, courtesy of the landlord, takes up little more of the afternoon. The youngsters are loud in their enjoyment; the erosion going on outside does not worry them in the least.

31

BETWEEN THE YEARS 1890 AND 1926
THE MAGGIA WASHED AN ANNUAL
AVERAGE OF 550,000 CUBIC METERS
OF DEBRIS INTO THE DELTA, THE
EQUIVALENT OF 55,000 LOADED
RAILROAD CARS!

(SEE "EROSION")

Chopping firewood with an ax, carrying a basketful of it into the living room, then lighting a fire in the grate, carrying one bucket after another up to the bathroom, taking care not to trip on the stairs with the scalding water, pouring bucket after bucket into the bathtub, which in half an hour is still not full, not even half full, so that the water always cools before there is enough for a bath, in the end it is not even lukewarm, and other irritations—

A small apartment in Basel would be more comfortable.

It was not to drink schnapps, but to buy matches, a reserve of matches, that Geiser had walked to the next village, and in the tavern he forgot to buy the matches.

Obviously brain cells are ceasing to function.

More serious than the collapse of a dry-stone wall would be a crack across the grounds, narrow at first, no broader than a hand, but a crack—

(That is the way landslides begin, cracks appearing noiselessly, not widening, or hardly at all, for weeks on end,

32

until suddenly, when one is least expecting it, the whole slope below the crack begins to slide, carrying even forests and all else that is not firm rock down with it.)

One must be prepared for everything.

For a moment, viewed through the window, it really looked like a crack no broader than a hand across the entire grounds—

Even field glasses can deceive.

When Geiser went out into the wet grounds to find out what he must be prepared for, it turned out to be a track made by the cat through the tall grass.

Autumn crocuses already in August.

A huge crack in the cliff behind the village, rising almost vertically up to the gray clouds, is from neither yesterday nor today; there are fir trees growing in it. A crack from gray, prehistoric ages. At no time within human memory has a village in this valley been overwhelmed, and in a place where rocks once fell, burying some farm buildings, no new building was ever erected. The local people know their valley.

What the field glasses reveal to him:

Walls of rock, stubborn as ever and always—

Not everything that Geiser described as granite in the first years—above all to his wife, but also to guests from the city who had no interest in stone—is in fact granite. Geiser has meanwhile come to know this, and not only through his son-in-law, who always knows everything.

Walls of rock, then, stone—

(Parts of them are indeed granite.)

An hour with the field glasses is enough to convince him that there is no new crack in the high and almost vertical cliff that is the only thing capable of burying the village; recent fractures would be lighter in color, gray and not faded like the whole rock face. The things that here and there looked at first glance like splits are shown up by the field glasses as black streaks on the smooth wall, discolorations caused by permanent rivulets, presumably algae. The ridge, the highest point, is admittedly hidden in the clouds; but Geiser knows it by heart: it is a sharp ridge free of loose debris, jagged for countless millennia, mountains that towered above the glaciers of the Ice Age, a trustworthy stone.

1)
COARSE, OCCASIONALLY PORPHYROID
GNEISS

2)
MICA-SCHIST ALTERNATING WITH GNEISS,
GRANITIC AND AMPHIBOLOGICAL ZONES,
WITH GRANULAR LIMESTONE (MARBLE)

It is idiotic to write out in one's own hand (in the evenings by candlelight) things already in print. Why not use scissors to cut out items that are worth remembering and deserve a place on the wall? Geiser is surprised that he did not think of this before. There are scissors in the house; all he has to do is find them. Quite apart from the fact that print is easier to read than an old man's handwriting— though he has taken the trouble to use block letters—no one has that much time.

Geological formations, layers that are clearly distinguished from the stratifications beneath and above them by the petrified animals and plants (see Characteristic Fossils) within them and that represent a (stratigraphic) unit. Among these belong the igneous rocks, which evolved at the same time. Related G. F. evolving successively are bracketed together in formation groups. Formations and formation groups reflect periods of the earth's history and are in consequence used as descriptions of time, the G. F. in the sense of periods, the formation groups in the sense of geological eras.

The glaciers of the Ice Age transformed these mountain ranges by acting on peaks and valleys according to new principles. Ravines, niches, sinkholes, cirques (basinlike hollows) were carved out at the head of the valleys, and the peaks, already shaped into ridges, sharpened still further. The massive rivers of ice transformed the valleys themselves into broad, U-shaped troughs. Large glaciers exerted more pressure than small ones, so that the main valleys generally lie deeper than the subsidiary ones. In many parts of the Alps individual mountains, all of them once covered with glaciers, reveal traces, not only of the grinding and polishing effect of glaciers, but also of erosion as a result of splitting or fracturing: round, knobbed slopes standing out against the sharp and jagged ridges that the glaciers left untouched, on flatter surfaces basins forming shallow lakes, features known as *roches moutonnées*, outcrops of rock with smooth reflecting surfaces, frequently striated by rough stones, scarred glacial scourings, here and there moraines in the form of dams, more often valley flanks adorned with moraines.

Such complicated structures are the result of prolonged development. Like all other mountain ranges formed in the same period (Alpine), this process extends over a whole series of geolog. formations and can be divided up into various fold-forming phases. The first orogenic movements occurred at the height of the Triassic period, also the Liassic. Several marked phases occurred in the Late Cretaceous and in the Tertiary, and movements have been continuing through the Diluvian (*see* Ice Age) up to the present day.

The diluvian ice sheet which rose even above the lower passes, leaving only the highest peaks jutting out like islands, did not begin to disappear until the arrival of the warm interglacial period, and disappeared completely only in the postglacial. It was then transformed into the present-day valley glaciers, hanging glaciers on the upper slopes, cirque glaciers in the hollows; a number of plateau glaciers have also been formed. This recent type of glaciation, now swiftly retreating, is responsible, along with the peak formations, the valleys and their openings, the crevices and ravines, the waterfalls cascading over the trough walls, and the lakes, for the remarkable scenic beauty of the Alps. The glacial undermining of the slopes combined with the disappearance of glacial buttressing has led to many landslides. The basinlike character of the trough valleys has been to some extent obliterated by erosion of the higher peaks and the consequent transfer of rock to the lower regions. This is the cause of marked silting in the larger valleys, where the mud flow frequently presents a danger to human settlements.

What Elsbeth would have said about these notes on the wall, growing daily more numerous, whether she would have put up with thumbtacks stuck in the paneling, is an idle question—

Geiser is a widower.

Not all the walls in the house are suitable for thumbtacks. These stick in the plaster only now and then and are by no means to be trusted; if one takes a hammer to them, they just buckle and fall to the floor, leaving holes in the white plaster, which would certainly not have entranced

37

Elsbeth, and all for nothing; not a single slip of paper remains on the wall. The best surface is paneling, in which a single thumbtack is enough, but only the living room is paneled—

Elsbeth would have shaken her head.

And this is only the beginning; the walls in the living room will provide nowhere near enough space, particularly since his paper slips must be affixed neither too high nor too low; otherwise, every time Geiser forgets what he so carefully cut out an hour ago, he will have to climb on a chair or crouch on his heels to read his pieces of paper. This is not only laborious, it also prevents an overall review, and once already the chair has nearly capsized. Where, for example, is the information about the conjectural brain of Neanderthal man? Instead, one finds oneself back with the drawing of the golden section. Where is the information about mutations, chromosomes, etc.? It is all so exasperating; Geiser is quite certain that there is an item somewhere about the quantum theory (as if it were not laborious enough, copying out texts full of foreign scientific words, sometimes even two or three times in order to get them right). What belongs where? Some slips, especially the larger ones, start to curl when they have been on the wall for a while; they refuse to lie flat. That presents another difficulty. To read them, one has to use both hands. Some curl at the bottom, others at the sides. There is nothing one can do about it. Each day they curl more and more (probably because of the humidity), and there is no glue in the house; otherwise he could stick them to the wall, though that would have the added disadvantage of making it impossible for him to substitute an item when a new and more important one was discovered. The golden section, for instance, is not all that important, and he can remember how many people there are in the canton of Ticino, how high the Matterhorn is (4,505 meters above sea level), or when the Vikings reached Iceland. He is not so decrepit as all that. The paper slips will lie flat only if one uses four thumbtacks on each, but his supply is not large. So they will just have to curl; when one opens a window, creating a draft, the whole wall flutters and rustles.

It is no longer a living room.

So far Geiser has hesitated to take down Elsbeth's portrait (in oil) from the wall to make room for more items. But now there is no other way.

> **Weakness of memory** is the deterioration of the faculty of recalling earlier experiences. In psychopathology a distinction is made between this and deterioration of the faculty of adding new experiences to the store of memories, though the distinction is only one of degree. In the brain diseases of old age (senility, hardening of the arteries in the brain) and other brain diseases, it is the latter faculty that deteriorates first.

Sometimes Geiser writes notes on things he believes he knows, without consulting an encyclopedia, things that also deserve a place on the wall, so that he will not forget them:

THE CELLS MAKING UP THE HUMAN
BODY, INCLUDING THE BRAIN,
CONSIST MAINLY OF WATER

THE EARTH IS NOT A PERFECT SPHERE

THERE HAS NEVER BEEN AN EARTH-
QUAKE IN TICINO

FISH DO NOT SLEEP

THE SUM TOTAL OF ENERGY IS
CONSTANT

HUMAN BEINGS ARE THE ONLY LIVING
CREATURES WITH AN AWARENESS OF
HISTORY

SNAKES HAVE NO HEARING

¾ OF THE EARTH'S SURFACE IS WATER

EUROPE AND AMERICA MOVE TWO
CENTIMETERS AWAY FROM EACH OTHER
EVERY YEAR, WHILE ENTIRE CONTINENTS
(ATLANTIS) HAVE ALREADY DISAPPEARED

SINCE WHEN HAVE WORDS EXISTED?

THE UNIVERSE IS EXPANDING

Sunday:

10:00 A.M.

Rain as cobwebs over the grounds.

10:40 A.M.

Rain as pearls on the windowpane.

11:30 A.M.

Rain as silence; not a bird twittering, not a dog barking in the village, the noiseless splashing in the puddles, raindrops gliding slowly down the wires.

11:50 A.M.

No rain.

1:00 P.M.

Rain invisible to the eye, but, stretching a hand out of the window, one feels it on one's skin.

3:10 P.M.

Rain as a hissing sound in the leaves of the chestnut tree.

3:20 P.M.

Rain like cobwebs.

4:00 P.M.

No rain, just the ivy dripping.

5:30 P.M.

Rain with wind, drumming on the windowpanes, splashing on the granite table outside; this now looks black, the splashes look like white narcissi.

6:00 P.M.

Gurgling sounds around the house again.

7:30 P.M.

No rain, but mist.

11:00 P.M.

Rain as a glittering in the beam of a flashlight.

At least it is not snowing.

In winter, when it is snowing, the valley is black. The blackness of the asphalt between the mounds of snow pushed aside by the snowplow. The blackness of footprints in the wet snow as it thaws, of wet granite. Snow plops down from the wires; the wires are black. Snow in the woods, snow on the ground and on branches, but the trunks are black. There is also snow on the roofs; the chimneys are black. Only the mail bus remains yellow; it has chains on its wheels, the track they leave is black. Here and there a red willow, almost the color of a fox, the bracken rusty, and when the streams are not frozen, the water black among snow-covered stones. The skies like ashes or lead; and the snow-covered mountains behind the black woods do not look white, just pale. All the birds black in flight. The undersides of the gutters are black with raindrops. The branches of the fir trees are green, but the fir cones look black against the snow. The crosses in the churchyard are mostly black. Even the sheep in the grounds are not white, but a dirty gray. A white snowman with a carrot for a nose, built for the grandchildren, stands on black moss. The shoes one afterward places beside the radiator are black with wet. When it is not snowing, one can often go walking without a coat, so warm is it at midday, Mediterranean skies; no foliage, one sees more of the rock than in summer, and when it is dry the rock looks silvery gray. The vines are bare, the slopes of dried-up bracken brown, interspersed with the white trunks of birch trees. It is only the nights that are cold, during the day the soil beneath the rustling leaves of autumn remains frozen, but it is sometimes possible at Christmas to drink coffee out of doors in the sunshine. The glaciers, which once stretched as far as Milan, are now in retreat everywhere; on the shadowed slopes the last rags of grimy snow have melted by May at the latest, even on the highest points. Just one ravine, which the sun` hardly ever reaches, retains the remnants of avalanches a little longer; but these vanish, too. All in all, a green valley. When the canton's yellow bulldozer comes along to widen the highway here and there, one can see moraine, debris from the huge glaciers of the Ice Age; the moraine so hard that it has to be blasted. Men blow three times on a little horn and wave a red flag, and shortly afterward the bits come rattling down, pebbles and gravel from the Ice Age.

> The village lies on a narrow ledge covered with ground moraine, the remains of a former valley bed that can be traced as far as Spruga.

This morning one can imagine for minutes on end that there is a shadow beneath the large fir tree—and at once two or three birds start twittering in the grounds; despite isolated showers, which glisten, it seems quite likely that the sun may suddenly burst through. The clouds, though they do not lift from the upper slopes, even during the afternoon, are fluffy and not really gray; indeed, here and there they show a bluish tint. Only the fir tree is still wet and black. All the same, one has the feeling of knowing just where the sun is behind the clouds, and for the first time in a week one can imagine that tomorrow or the day after (what is one day more or less?) the sun will be shining.

The sound of rushing waters is still coming from the ravine.

But in the evening, when Geiser returns to the window to look out for the moon, gray vapors are rising once more from the lower valley. It is not raining, but clouds keep drifting across; some break up into ragged wisps against the slopes and vanish again, but others do not. A quarter of an hour later the fir tree is no longer to be seen.

TRAINS WITH CONNECTIONS IN BELLINZONA

LOCARNO	BASEL
0943	1426
1157	1616
1548	2019
1806	22 27
2329	04 12

The valley has only the one highway, which has many curves but is protected almost everywhere by iron railings; a narrow but good highway that unnerves only foreigners, particularly Dutchmen. Fatal accidents are much rarer than one would think when seeing this highway for the first time. The constant awareness of ravines on the one side, and rocks with sharp edges on the other, the feeling that the iron railings would not resist the impact of a car, encourages drivers to be cautious and alert. When two cars are unable to pass, the driver coming from above must back his vehicle up to a place where he can pull over. An old laborer takes care of the highway year after year, cutting back the proliferating bracken on the slopes, clearing away the stones that have fallen on the asphalt, in the fall sweeping up the wet leaves. State and canton do everything to ensure that the valley does not die; mail bus thrice daily.

All in all, no deserted valley.

There are snakes, grass snakes, which are harmless, and various kinds of vipers, among them asps, but whole summers can go by without one's seeing even a grass snake, one just hears a rustling in the nettles. The valley is swarming with lizards, which are also harmless; they bask on the stone window sills and flit up and down the walls of the house. There are no longer any bears or wild boars, foxes are rare, and there are not even rumors of wolves. Summer visitors from the big cities, claiming to have seen an eagle on their rambles, cannot be taken seriously; the last eagle observed over this valley is now hanging in the smoky saloon of a tavern, where it has been since the First World War. Higher up the slopes there are said to be marmots. Cows are few and far between; since the slopes are too steep, it is more a valley for sheep and goats and hens.

Garbage collecting is a recent innovation.

Only a short while ago people were still throwing their rubbish down the slope beside the church: bottles, old rags, cans and worn-out shoes, boxes, pans, stockings, etc., some of which got caught in the bushes.

The local people are Catholics.

There is little to suggest that the valley might once have been occupied by the Romans. No Roman paving stones, let alone the remains of an arena. Forest and debris had no appeal for the medieval overlords, either; they preferred to set up their strongholds down on the plain or beside the lakes, where ownership was more rewarding. No Visconti or Sforza has ever trodden this valley. No robber baron has left even a tower behind. No place name commemorates a victory or a defeat, neither Hannibal nor Suvorov came this way.

A valley without through traffic.

Now and again one hears the flickering sound of a helicopter transporting building materials; somewhere construction work is still going on.

Otherwise little happens.

In earlier times the people lived by basket work, a cottage industry using child labor, but then cheap Japanese work took over the market in Milan.

The young people leave the valley.

There are no plans for a reservoir.

It is almost impossible to find a local person to mow a pensioner's lawn. Even grass has lost its value. All the same, the price of land is rising here, too; owning land makes one feel safer, even when there is no profit to be made from it. Figs do not ripen, but grapes do. Many of the chestnut trees are cankered. In the fall men come to cut them down, one hears the whine of their power saws for days on end, though one never sees the men working in the woods.

All in all, a quiet valley.

What Geiser values most is the air, the absence of industry. The streams are as unpolluted as in the Middle Ages. Perhaps one might come upon a rotting mattress in some inaccessible gorge; but as a rule the water could be drunk safely.

BANDITA DI CACCIA/HUNTING PROHIBITED

Hunting is controlled by law.

CADUTA DI MASSI/FALLING ROCKS

This refers to the fragments of rock one occasionally sees on the asphalt; not to landslides; the slopes have a safe and solid gradient, and the ridges above remain as they always were. The glaciers have been retreating for centuries. The last patches of grimy snow in the shadows have all melted by July or August at the latest. The beds of the streams have not changed within living memory, and are large enough to cope with heavy storms. A fireplace beside the stream, built at one time by his grandchildren, vanished the following year, swept away by high water, but the hollows and indents in the rock which turn the water into foam, the large slabs, covered only when the water rises to flood level, and the sharp-edged boulders remain unchanged from year to year, though the bright and smooth round pebbles are presumably different ones.

Erosion is a slow process.

Now and again in summer a tent can be seen, yellow or blue, a car with a German license plate standing under a tree in some unexpected place, and people, tourists, bathing in the stream. But if one climbs up to the heights one no longer runs into contemporaries; one comes to the ruins of stone barns, roofs collapsed but the four walls still standing, within them a tangle of nettles beneath an open sky, and nothing stirring. No dogs barking. Other barns, not yet in ruins, have doors standing open; inside there may still be a faint smell of hay, the goat dung is dry, almost petrified. No bones of former inhabitants lying around. The water troughs, also of granite, are empty and dry, the faucet rusted, the view splendid, no different from thousands of years ago. Here and there a small chapel; a faded Virgin Mary behind rusty wire netting, a rusty can containing withered flowers in front of it, frescoes under the porch eaves, some of them spoiled, since the goats have been licking the walls for saltpeter.

A valley with no Baedeker stars.

At the end of the valley, where the highway stops, there are Italian border guards, youngsters from Palermo and Messina, standing with their hands in the pockets of their uniforms, glad when some woodcutter or angler stops to talk to them. These days smuggling is not profitable in untracked mountain areas. At the end of the valley there are some quarries, now and again a blasting operation, a series of explosions, then a cloud of dust over the forest; shortly afterward, trucks drive down the valley, loaded with squared stones or slabs. Panning for gold in the streams has never been worth the trouble. In summer there are cranberries, also mushrooms. When it is not raining, the white trails of passenger planes can be seen high up in the blue sky above the mountains, though one does not hear them. The last murder in the valley—and that only rumored, since it never came to court—happened whole decades ago. Ever since the young men have owned motorcycles, incest has been dying out, and so has sodomy.

Women have had the vote since 1971.

One summer the woodpeckers got a sudden idea, as it were: they stopped pecking the bark of the old chestnut tree and started on the windowpanes; more and more of them came, all seemingly obsessed by glass. Not even strips of glittering foil frightened them off for long. It became a real nuisance. If one went to the window to shoo them away, they at once moved to another, and one could not be at every window, clapping one's hands. Geiser found it more effective to strike the granite table with a lath, which made a sound like the crack of a shotgun—then they flew off to wait in the surrounding branches. Later one would hear them again at some window or other; they could not get a grip on the smooth glass, and with their wings fluttering they could tap on the pane only two or three times, occasionally but rarely even four times. By the following summer they had forgotten all about it. Twice a week a blonde butcher woman drives the length of the valley, selling meat from her Volkswagen; she is of German extraction, married to a man from Ticino. Fishing produces very little. Many of the chestnut trees are cankered, but all in all it is a green valley, wooded as in the Stone Age. The bracken grows almost head-high. In August, when it is not raining, there are shooting stars to be seen, or one hears the call of a little owl. When there is mist in the lower valley, the moonlight on the mist can give the effect of a lake with jagged bays, a fjord; all it would need is a ship lying at anchor below the village, a black cutter or a whaler.

> Before the highway was constructed in 1896, the mule track, built in 1768 by the Remonda brothers from Comologno at their own expense, provided the only connection between the Valle Onsernone and the outside world.

> Despite the basic poverty of the soil, the shortsightedness of the provincial government, the damage done to communities through the continual partitionings and lootings perpetrated by the French, Austrian, and Russian armies at the time of the French Revolution and under Napoleon I, the people of Ticino performed veritable miracles in constructing good and practical highways; these extended from Chiasso to Airolo, from Brissago to the Lukmanier Pass; they even penetrated into the adjacent valleys and up the slopes of the steepest mountains, bringing the remotest Alpine villages into contact with civilization.

In Iceland there are moraines from the late Ice Age that are still not overgrown, whole valleys full of rock debris that will never be anything but desert. There, one would be lost without a Land Rover. Glaciers overhang the sea. One of these, VATNAJÖKUL, is larger than all the Alpine glaciers together. There are rows of volcanoes, cones of

ash; it is possible to climb them, only to find oneself looking down on a different kind of desert, where even a Land
Rover is of no use, a desert of black and brown and mauve
lava. No trees. What looks from a distance like a green
oasis is usually a moor. One can drive for days without
seeing a farm; now and again a few isolated sheep, what
grows amid the debris is not enough to feed a herd. When
one steps outside the tent at night, there is not a single
light on land to be seen. Not a sound. During the day
there are birds, many birds. When the sun shines, as it
does once in a while, the flat crowns of the unending
glaciers gleam in the distance. Usually all there is to see is
clouds, beneath them the gravelly plains. Here and there
on the plains large stones can be made out, round and
smooth, lying just as the Ice Age glaciers shaped them.
The weather changes from hour to hour, but the desert
remains as it is, simply changing color—and there is no
color that cannot be seen at some time during the long
days. The wheel tracks left in the gravel or mud by one's
own vehicle provide the only sign that there are people
on our planet. There are flowers, small ones, as in the
Alps, all kinds of moss and lichen. Elsewhere, a hissing
on the surface, a greenish bubbling and splashing between
crusts of yellow, and a smell of sulfur. There are whole
ravines and hollows stained with sulfur, elsewhere a plain
covered with clouds of white steam, somewhere else a waterfall. A broad river of glacier water tumbles down over a
slab of basalt or a series of slabs, a thundering cascade of
gray water; the wet basalt glistens like bronze, and a cloud
of spray can be seen for miles, accompanied by a rainbow.
The rain, when it comes, does not last very long. A blue
sky is a rare sight. The clouds lie low over the highlands

and drift along the glaciers, turning them gray, and all one sees of the sky is a yellow stripe along the horizon, the color of amber or lemon, and toward midnight lilac. Dawn follows almost immediately, in the distance a reddish dust, a sandstorm. Somewhere else rivers tracing a shining network of veins across the plain. There are fjords without a single ship, without a single living soul, except for a young seal. No farm, not even an abandoned one, nowhere the works of man. Surf around a black tower of lava; the cone of ash has been washed away. Encircling the fjord, the horizontal mountains, identical slabs of basalt; the slopes down to the sea are green. A world before the creation of man. In many places it is impossible to guess in what era one is. But seagulls have already been created, their fluttering wings over the pale and leaden sea white against the ink-blue clouds. As a rule there are no icebergs visible, but the sea is icy. Despite the Gulf Stream. Strips of old snow, and not only on the northern slopes; summer does not last long enough to melt them. Despite the excessively long days. If the Arctic ice were to melt, New York would be under water. A sign that the Creation has already taken place is a lighthouse, somewhere else an American radar station. Here and there driftwood from Siberia. Beneath the deep clouds the sea is black with varying patches of quicksilver, for an hour it looks as blue as the Mediterranean, at midnight like mother of pearl. There are volcanoes covered with glaciers, HEKLA, the only volcano now emitting smoke. Another volcano, a new one, has risen from the sea, an island of ash and basalt; its first inhabitants, when the ash cools, are birds that feed on fish; their excrement will form the beginning of an oasis in which human beings can live, until the next stream of lava smothers it all. Probably the fish will outlive us, and the birds.

Man, Latin *homo*. Gr. *anthropos* (see illustration, p. 685, and tables, pp. 676 and 684).

1) *Man's singularity.* Man has always been conscious of the mystery surrounding his origin and development as a species, and an inexhaustible field of inquiry is opened to him by his ability to regard himself (the "subject") in relation to the world in which he lives (the "object")—*see* Philosophy. This objective attitude toward the world is what gives M. his ability to conquer it, and is thus responsible for his special status in the universe.

Since M. is unable to understand himself through insight, he has from earliest times tried to reach out toward the idea of a divine being (*see* Religion) or some other nonhuman presence, to which he equates himself while at the same time distinguishing himself from it; it may be an animal (*see* Totemism), the spirit of an ancestor (*see* Ancestor Worship), or some other alter ego (*see* Mask); in rationalistic times it might even be a machine (LAMETTRIE: *L'Homme machine*).

That M. is a *historical being* is shown in the fact that he is shaped, both outwardly and inwardly, by inherited skills, arts, sciences, customs, standards of conduct, and value systems; toward these he adopts a critical attitude, which he then complements, improves, simplifies, complicates, modifies, and alters. Additionally, he is able to envisage different states of being and to plan these deliberately, to provide himself with purposes and aims, through the use of his productive imagination and will. The more highly developed animals display hopes and fears, but only M. works toward a "future."

Such abilities are brought about by a retrogressive metamorphosis of those fixed, innate behavior patterns which in animals we refer to as "instinct." M. does not live as an integral part of his natural environment, finding his bearings through instinct; his intelligence, his actions, and his labor enable him to modify and adapt his environment. This provides scope for innumerable varieties of behavior inimical to his survival, for errors and aberrations of planning and purpose, but despite this M. has succeeded in spreading his species across the entire globe and adapting his way of life to diverse conditions. He has transformed large areas of the earth's surface to meet his needs, and the proportion of civilized areas in the world is constantly increasing.

There have been some landslides; not here, but farther up the valley. It looks chaotic, he has been told: the stream has altered course, the birch grove has vanished, simply been swept away, the valley bed covered entirely with debris. Geiser knows the place from rambles with his grandchildren, but now, he is told, it is unrecognizable, the iron bridge leading to the saw mill gone, and no longer necessary anyway, since the stream has changed course. The road has disappeared. The saw mill, of which a third has been destroyed, is now on the left bank of the stream instead of the right, and the ground floor, where all the machines are kept, is full of pebbles and sand, the stream full of tree trunks, their bark torn away by the stones, and sheet iron. Nothing is left but a bare passage, the slopes stripped of trees and soil, from top to bottom nothing but naked rock; it looks chaotic.

There has been no loss of life.

Who could have told him that? Only the parish clerk Francesco, who came along yesterday to borrow his field glasses; apart from him Geiser has not seen anybody in the past few days.

CHE TEMPO, CHE TEMPO!

The old bridge over the Isorno is also said to have gone, which means that the former mule track is cut; an arch slung from rock to rock at least ten meters above the stream, a construction that has held for centuries; presumably the narrow gorge became blocked by tree trunks, which caused the water to pile up.

And it is still raining.

The German solar investigator has not returned; Geiser finds this quite understandable; a scholar cannot help being bored by the questions of a layman who finds the idea of curved space impossible to grasp but continues to ask questions. And in any case, he does not want anyone to come into the house and see his papers on the wall.

ALWAYS BE PREPARED.

SPEED OF LIGHTNING: 100,000 KILO-
METERS PER SECOND. INTENSITY OF
CURRENT: 20 TO 180,000 AMPERES

The power is on again, and there is Geiser, candle in hand, unable to remember why he has his hat on.

The hot plate is glowing.

Light in the cellar, too.

Geiser has not forgotten that the deepfreeze, which is humming again, is empty, and he also remembers why he has his hat on: he meant to go to the post office. No point in the hat; he had forgotten that the highway is blocked and no mail is getting through. There is no point in the candle, either, since the power is on again.

One always forgets something.

Who told him about the damage in the valley?

While Geiser is failing to remember where he put the candle in case the power should go off again, the hot plate continues to glow; unfortunately the soup left there for warming, the minestrone, has gone sour; there is no point in the hot plate.

There have been some landslides—

Geiser now remembers what he was looking for in the closet—sealing wax—and as he at last turns the glowing hot plate off, he also remembers why he went into the kitchen instead of searching in the closet; he saw the hot plate glowing, evidently the power has been on again for some time.

Geiser is still wearing his hat.

The clock is also striking again.

3:00 P.M.

While Geiser is wondering why he wanted a candle in the middle of the afternoon, he remembers having intended to seal a document, his final instructions in case anything happened. His resolve, as he searches for a pan, is to clean out his closet one of these days. But the pan, the little one, is already standing on the hot plate, the water in it bubbling, though the hot plate is no longer glowing. He forgot, while thinking about the untidiness of his closet and about his heirs, that he had already drunk his tea; the empty cup is warm, the tea bag dark and wet.

In the closet he discovers:

income-tax documents, a land-registry plan of his property, receipts, the key for a Fiat that ceased to exist years ago, his polytechnic diploma, letters of all kinds that are no concern of his heirs, and an out-of-date X-ray picture of his spine, his gray ribs, his white hip bones, plus sealing wax, but no seal; and there is also something else he cannot find—his passport.

It is 4:00 P.M.

At the moment he does not need his passport, but he could do with an aspirin for his headache, which is not raging, just irritating, and it would also be a good time to clean out his medicine chest, to throw away all the things of which he no longer knows the use: whether for itching or for acid in the urine, for heart troubles or for constipation, for gnat bites or for sunburn, etc.

A spotted salamander in the bathroom—

When Geiser sees in the mirror that he is still wearing his hat, he remembers where his passport is.

The headache is gradually fading.

The spotted salamander must have fallen in through the open window, and since it cannot climb up again on the smooth tiles, it is just lying there, black with yellow spots, motionless. One does not feel like touching it, though spotted salamanders are harmless. When Geiser prods it gently with the toe of his shoe, it just kicks out with all fours. Quite automatically. Then it goes quiet again, its skin armored, black with yellow spots, and slimy. The cat, Kitty, does not touch the salamander, either, but begins instead to rub against his trouser legs as soon as he returns to the kitchen.

The hot plate is turned off.

Cats always fall on their feet, but in spite of that she is now yowling outside the front door; perhaps Geiser said: Get out—but after that not a word in the house.

Outside it is raining.

There is no ladder in the house.

It is true the gray cobwebs on the ceiling have been there a long time; but when one becomes conscious of them, one finds no rest; an ordinary broom is not long enough, since the ceiling above the stairs is too high, and one cannot set a chair on the stairs.

Geiser finds no time for reading.

Some time later the spotted salamander is lying on the carpet in the living room, and that is a repulsive sight. Geiser picks it up with the small shovel and throws it into the grounds, but the cobwebs are still there above the stairs. There is only one way of getting them down: unscrew the long handrail of the banisters, then attach a little broom to the handrail with wire—

Kitty is still yowling outside the front door.

The cobwebs are gone.

Water in the cellar, but that is not what Geiser went to the cellar to inspect; he had already seen it. There, all of a sudden, are the pliers, but no idea now what he wanted them for an hour ago. Instead, Geiser remembers the men in blue overalls and the tip he gave them, and he does not need to check whether the tank is filled with heating oil.

It can get cold in September.

Some time later, when his eyes again fall on the bent nail in the wall, he has no idea where he put the pliers.

The bent nail has to go.

In the process the scissors break.

Everything is breaking; yesterday the thermometer, today the banisters: the old screws refuse to return to their rusty sockets, and lining the stairs is now nothing but a row of upright posts without a handrail.

Man remains an amateur.

The spotted salamander on the carpet in the living room must have been another one; the first is still lying in the bathroom, black with yellow spots, and slimy.

The magnifying glass is in his rucksack.

Actually Geiser meant to take a bath, since the water is hot again, following his fruitless work on the banisters; it made him sweat, and his hands are covered with rust from the screws.

It would be time for the news.

When one examines a spotted salamander through a magnifying glass, it looks like a monster: a dinosaur. Its overlarge head, the black, unfocused eyes. Suddenly it moves. Its clumsy walk, rather in the style of someone doing push-ups, tail held rigid. It crawls doggedly in a direction in which it will never make any progress. Suddenly it lies still again, its head raised. One can see its pulse beating. An awful dullness in all limbs.

Salamander: member of the amphibian family Salamandridae. Land S.: 1) spotted or fire S. (*S. salamandra*); 2) black or alpine S. (*S. atra*). Water S.: *see* Newt.

Newt: tailed amphibian of the family Salamandridae (*q.v.*).

Salamandridae: amphibian family that includes salamanders and newts. The distinguishing mark of the newt is its tail, which is laterally compressed, whereas the salamander has a round tail. Both forms occur in Europe, and all possess 4 fingers and 5 toes. The spotted salamander (*S. salamandra*), black and yellow in color, occurs in two forms, spotted and striped, and varies in length from 10 to 20 centimeters. The black or alpine salamander (*S. atra*) is entirely black. The commonest varieties of newt are the common or spotted N. (*Triton vulgaris*), the great or crested N. (*T. cristatus*), and the alpine N. (*T. alpestris*). The crested N. is distinguished by the notched crest that comes into prominence in the spring; the male of this species attains a length of 13 to 15 centimeters, whereas the common N. is rarely more than half that length.

Amphibia: cold-blooded vertebrates capable of living either on land or in water. Most of them lay eggs in water, and after hatching, the young undergo a process of metamorphosis (*q.v.*), passing through a tadpole stage, in which they breathe through gills, later replaced by lungs. Some A., however, are viviparous. A. are divided into 4 orders: (1) *Apoda* (limbless and snakelike); (2) *Urodela* (usually with 4 limbs and a tail, e.g., salamanders, newts); (3) *Anura* (4 limbs but no tail, e.g., frogs, toads); and (4) *Stegocephali*, an extinct, lizardlike order, existing from the Carboniferous to the Triassic and reaching a length of several meters. The largest amphibia still in existence are the Goliath frog (*Rana goliath*) of Africa and the giant salamander of Japan (*Megalobatrachus japonicus*), which can attain a length of more than 1 meter.

Amphibia
Micropholis Stowi: skeleton, seen from above. Early mid-Triassic

Whether the spotted or alpine salamanders of today can be regarded as the successors of dinosaurs or as an early form of them is not clear from the encyclopedia.

SAURISCHIA:
GREEK: SAUROS = LIZARD
DINOSAURS:
GREEK: DEINOS = TERRIBLE

Since the scissors, the usual ones, broke, Geiser has been using nail scissors, and after the thumbtacks have been used up, there is still a whole reel of tape, Magic Tape, which sticks on wall plaster.

THE ERA OF THE DINOSAURS

Huge and grotesque as the Saurischia of the earth's middle period were, the golden age of the dinosaurs was still to come. During the Jurassic and Carboniferous periods the warm seas rose and engulfed a large part of Europe and almost half of North America. Corals built their reefs up to 3,000 kilometers farther north than their present outposts. Fig and breadfruit trees flourished in Greenland, palms in Alaska. And the terrible cold-blooded dinosaurs also moved north and, amazingly, flourished everywhere.

In the luxuriant swamps and stagnant lakes these huge herbivores of the Saurischia family made their homes amid the tall grasses and the bracken. "In armor clad, by steel surrounded, The host which many a nation doomed; As they advanced, the earth resounded, As they passed, the thunder boomed." Goethe might almost have intended these words from his *Faust* to apply to these monsters, for beneath the footsteps of such giants, ten to eleven times heavier than the elephant of today, the earth must indeed have boomed like thunder. In order to bear their own enormous weight they had once again taken to all four limbs; their legs were veritable pillars, monolithic in size and strength. Opinions have long been divided over the manner

63

in which these walking mountains of flesh deployed their clumsy legs—whether, like crocodiles, bent scissorlike, allowing their bellies to drag along the ground and only occasionally raising themselves up, or, in the manner of the hoofed giants of today, such as elephants, bearing the weight principally on the massive hind legs, splaying the front legs slightly outward from the elbows, like a bulldog. Everything points toward the latter interpretation. These giants were so heavy that they could only have lived half-submerged in swamps and shallow lakes, where the water would help to carry their weight. The prototype of this titanic family was the *Brontosaurus*, the "thunder lizard"— weighing about 30 tons, and more than 20 meters in length. Its tiny head, hardly more than a slight swelling at the front end of its snakelike neck, contained a few spoon-shaped teeth and a small, primitive brain, which probably had little to do except control the jaws and interpret the weak impressions conveyed to it by the monster's very limited senses. The hind legs were controlled by a relatively large nerve center located far back in the base of the spine; this was much bigger than the sparrowlike brain in its head.

It was, however, with the development of the amazing *Tyrannosaurus rex* that the dinosaurs reached their apex; no more terrible and powerful carnivore has ever arisen to terrorize the earth. Gigantic both in size and in strength, this awe-inspiring creature, 15 meters long and almost 6 meters high, moved on massive hind legs, each equipped with three toes and horrible claws. Its main weapon of attack lay in its murderous jaws, with saber-shaped fangs 15 centimeters long. Although these true tyrants among the dinosaurs had nothing to fear anywhere on earth, their reign was of short duration. They first emerged in the Late Cretaceous and vanished—along with all the other dinosaurs—at the end of this period, when they were suddenly and inexplicably wiped out.

64

Luckily it was his reading glasses, and not the others, that fell on the kitchen floor and broke. That would have been a worse disaster, for it makes one dizzy to gaze at everything through reading glasses. And, if necessary, one can always use the magnifying glass for reading.

Plesiosaurs: extinct group of reptiles with elongated necks (e.g., *Elasmosaurus*), short tails, and paddle-shaped limbs. Complete skeletons discovered in Germany and England, partic. in lias.

Ichthyornis (approx. 1/6 life size)

Ichthyosaurs (Gk. fish-lizard): extinct order of aquatic reptiles living in the sea during Mesozoic times, particularly the Jurassic. Their body was fishlike, with a large caudal fin, and the caudal vertebrae continued into the lower lobe of the double tail fin, shaped like a shark's. The skull had a long beak with numerous conical teeth, and the eyes were surrounded by sclerotic plates; the limbs were well adapted for use as steering paddles. Up to 15 meters in length, they were viviparous. Their diet consisted mainly of fish and cuttlefish.

To keep on looking at one's wristwatch, just in order to convince oneself that time is passing, is absurd. Time has never yet stood still just because a person is bored and stands at the window, not knowing what he is thinking. The last time Geiser looked at his watch it was six o'clock—or, more exactly, three minutes to six.

And now?

—one minute to six.

There is always something one can do.

So one would imagine.

The portrait of Elsbeth that he recently took from the wall and put in the hallway is out of place there. Where should it go? This indicates that, since last looking at his watch, Geiser has been in the hallway; otherwise the portrait would not be in his hands, and he is now standing in the bedroom.

Presumably his watch has stopped.

The portrait of Elsbeth, depicting the nineteen-year-old daughter of an executive in the chemical industry, and painted by a local artist who has since become famous, has no place in the bedroom, either; it shows a face Geiser never knew, and the eyes do not look at one; the best place for it would be an art gallery, where these days it would be considered valuable.

—that is what Geiser was thinking.

The Basel art gallery is famous.

For the time being it is standing behind the bureau.

When Geiser goes back to the window to convince himself, by watching the slowly gliding raindrops, that time is not standing still—and in the whole of history it has never done that!—and when he cannot resist looking at his watch again, it reads seven minutes past six.

Somewhere a tapping on metal again.

The other noise:

Footsteps in the house, his own—

There is still firewood in the basket beside the grate, all Geiser needs to do to start a fire is to crumple up an old newspaper and stuff it beneath the firewood, put a heavier log on that, lean another against it, and finally a weighty branch, still with its bark, on top—

So now that has been done, too.

For someone to climb on a chair, attach a rope to a beam on the ceiling, and hang himself, in order to escape the sound of his own footsteps—this is something Geiser finds it possible to imagine.

However, it is no longer six o'clock.

This evening will also pass.

At the moment Geiser is standing before his gallery of papers, hands in pockets, and the fire is crackling.

A forked branch like that will glow for hours—

As far as Geiser knows, it is doubtful whether there are any people on Mars; probably there are whole Milky Ways without a trace of brain matter.

A night without rain—

Despite this, Geiser cannot sleep. His rucksack is packed, the flashlight back in the rucksack, the magnifying glass, too, though actually he needs it again now. To read. He has not yet gone to bed, though it is already midnight. The tapping on metal has stopped. When he holds his breath, not a sound can be heard, nothing except his own pulse. There is still a glow in the fireplace. Geiser has no desire for sleep; a person does not have all that much time—

Geology is a science devoted to tracing the development of the earth through its various eras since the formation of the earth's crust, and it covers a period of 2,000 million years—according to recent discoveries, 5,000 million years (*see* Geological Eras). The eras vary considerably in length; the Paleozoic, for instance, lasted 340 million years, the Mesozoic 140 million, and the Cainozoic 60 million. Geology embraces the history of the lithosphere (land and sea), volcanic phenomena, and the world of plants and animals. One recognizable feature is the frequent recurrence of the process by which geosynclines become filled with deposits, which are then transformed by orogenesis into firm masses; these tend generally to form continents, which are then exposed to erosion by endogenous and exogenous forces. Organic life originated some 1,500 million years ago, but the first traces are discernible only in rocks dating back some 1,000 million years; the trend has been toward the evolution of higher stages and a greater variety of forms, along with improved quality. In this process the changing pattern of the earth has played an important role, making it imperative for plants and animals to adapt to new living conditions, to migrate, or to die out.

At dawn, before the brief peal from the church bell, Geiser took his packed rucksack, his hat, raincoat, and umbrella, and left the house. The rucksack is not too heavy, and by the time he reaches the woods his heart has stopped pounding. In the village there is nobody to catch sight of him and ask where Herr Geiser is going, climbing the mountain with his rucksack in this weather.

Geiser knows what he is doing.

The pass lies 1,076 meters above sea level, and Geiser knows the way, at any rate as far as the top of the pass, from expeditions in previous years; besides, he has a map; he knows that one must keep to the left where the path forks, and that there are barns along the route in which one can shelter in case of a heavy thunderstorm, and more barns on the pass itself—

A path is a path even in fog.

At least there has been no thunder.

The path is not steep at the beginning; the slope is steep, but the path is almost horizontal, parts of it covered with slabs, a safe path even in fog, when óne can hear the roar of the waterfall though one might not see it.

Farther on, the path grows steeper.

Later, Geiser gives up looking out for a chapel—below the path, to the right, if memory serves; perhaps it was invisible in the fog.

The woods must begin to thin sometime.

He has forgotten whether the path leads over two or over three bridges before it leaves the woods. When one can hear a stream close by, even if it cannot be seen, one ought in spite of the fog to be able to make out the railings of a bridge—or perhaps he just crossed a bridge without noticing it—

The high bridge has railings.

(Unless it has been swept away!)

The field glasses jogging against his chest are not really heavy, only useless. All he can see in the fog: the nearest tree trunks (their foliage hidden in fog), bracken, a few meters of the path ahead, somewhere a red bench, rocks indicating a gorge, then, all of a sudden, the railings.

The tubular uprights are twisted.

After one hour precisely Geiser takes his first rest, though he does not remove his rucksack or sit down. The climb is of course more laborious than in previous years, but his heart stops pounding.

He has plenty of time.

Many of the slabs that form the path look very heavy; it must have been hard work finding all these slabs, dragging them to the right spot, and fixing them in such a way that the path would stand firm in all storms—the trouble he himself is having with them, treading step by step from one to the next, is nothing by comparison; at times the steps are rather too high, which robs one of breath and proves discouraging.

The umbrella is a nuisance.

Now and again the path forks, but none of these can be the fork marked on the map, and Geiser feels no need yet to consult his map: the important fork, at which he must veer left, is somewhere above the first barns, and Geiser has not yet seen any barns. Despite this, he feels briefly unsure of himself—perhaps the fog prevented him from seeing the barns—until he realizes that it was only a short cut; the paths, both the steeper and the other one, come together again, so going back and taking the steeper path was a waste of effort after all.

The day is still young.

Even if in the fog it is impossible to know exactly where one is, the path is leading upward at every curve; the important thing is to keep going, without haste, step by step, regularly and without haste, so as never to run short of breath.

The barns at last—

A silly dog barking.

After half an hour, earlier than planned, Geiser takes another rest, without removing his rucksack, no desire for Ovomaltine; however, he does sit down on a mossy rock, drenched through in spite of his umbrella, but confident:

His plan is workable.

At the fork—the other path leads to a spring pasture, to a group of houses on the farther side of the valley, where, according to the map, it comes to an end—he chose correctly, also at a second fork not shown on the map. A white-red-white mark on a rock confirmed it. Later, the path became narrower, and it had no slabs.

Geiser has made two resolutions:

1. to keep to a path at all times,
2. to give up at any sign of heart trouble, and on no account to exhaust himself.

Once already Geiser has tripped over a root branch; a little blood on his skin, mixed with rain, a graze on his right arm, in which he is holding the umbrella, but not enough to make it necessary to undo his rucksack for a bandage. A walking stick would have been more useful than the umbrella, an oilskin better than the gabardine raincoat, which becomes heavy when wet.

The rain has not eased up.

An unbridged stream—not a proper stream, but a stretch of flowing water that is just the result of persistent rain and is not marked on the map, water flowing over debris, wide, but nowhere so deep or swift that one could not wade it in knee-high boots—this has cost him a lot of time, since Geiser is wearing ordinary walking shoes. Half an hour at least. He walked up the slope and then down it, looking for stones he could trust, stones as large as possible, which would not tip or roll over when he set foot on them, and close enough for him to step across. But it was more or less the same everywhere. In the end there was nothing left but to risk it. One of the stones in which, after lengthy examination, he put his particular trust did then tip over— he did not fall, but he got a shoe full of water. This happened at nine in the morning, that is to say, while the day was still young.

Nearer the pass the ground becomes more even—

Ten years ago (Geiser is now approaching seventy-four) and in sunshine, it had been just a pleasant walk, an outing of two and a half hours there and back.

His memory has served him correctly:

a wide pass, pastures, rectangular dry-stone walls, and woods with clearings, the trees mostly deciduous (though beeches, not birches), and a few scattered houses (not barns, but deserted summer houses), and the path disappears in the open pastures, as is usual.

It would be time for a rest.

The thought that nobody could possibly know where Herr Geiser is at this particular moment pleases him.

No cattle—

No birds—

Not a sound—

To survey the landscape and find out before taking his rest what still lay ahead of him—the map shows a path with plenty of crosshatching, which means rock—Geiser went on farther. No path, and no view down into the other valley, just woods, growing ever steeper, undergrowth covering mossy debris, on which he kept stumbling, and in the end he found himself unable to move without slipping. Besides the gasping for breath there was now anxiety, haste, irritation with himself, and sweat, and where the undergrowth began to thin, the slope became even steeper; it was scarcely possible for him to remain upright. His progress turned into a crawling on all fours, an hour of which can use up more energy than three hours on a path, from one root branch to the next, and suddenly great walls of rock—

One false step and it is all over.

Geiser would not be the first.

Suddenly it has all become a question of luck.

By the time Geiser regains the open pasture of the pass, glad that there has been nobody to see him, it is noon. A gray noon. Beneath a large fir tree, where the ground is almost dry, though unfortunately teeming with ants, Geiser changes out of his sweaty shirt and waits for his confidence to return, his self-reliance, the feeling of not being lost.

He is not conscious of hunger.

A year ago two younger people, who had also lost their way, were not discovered for three weeks, even by a helicopter; it was only when someone noticed a number of birds circling over the woods, always in the same spot, that they were found.

Geiser has forgotten his Thermos.

The weather does not seem to worry the red ants in the least; their silent industry in a heap of fir needles—

He could do with his afternoon nap.

When one is not moving, one begins to feel chilly. Geiser has changed out of his wet socks as well, but his wet trouser legs still feel like cold poultices.

He has not forgotten the map, however.

The path leading seven hundred meters downward on the other side of the pass, to the right of the gorge according to the map, is bound to be a steep one, and when Geiser gets up to put on his rucksack, he feels the wobble in his knees. However, it has stopped raining. For a while, walking over the open pasture lands, he is not sure what he may decide to do.

Aurigeno/Valle Maggia

Not far from the place where, three hours ago, Geiser was lost in the undergrowth, he sees this inscription on a rock in white paint, with an arrow pointing to the path, which leads right through the beech trees. A narrow path, stony in places, then one is again walking on woodland soil, which is kinder to wobbly knees, and as long as one does not tread on the roots, which are slippery in the wet, it is an innocuous path. In the woods one cannot see the gray clouds, the foliage is green, the ferns green, and to turn back, as Geiser was contemplating during his rest, would have been silly.

His plan is workable.

Geiser had figured on five to six hours (his son-in-law claims it took him just two and a half hours), making allowances for his age.

The first gully is nothing to worry about.

The second looks more troublesome, a steep hollow filled with debris, a tangled mass of boulders and shattered tree trunks, rivulets but no raging streams, one trudges through pebbles and mud, holding on to a rotting branch or a rock, not without some palpitations—but in the end one finds the path again. The warning in the guidebook ("Descen

via the Valle Lareccio: care needed in bad weather")
seems somewhat exaggerated when one is actually there,
even though the slope is getting steeper and steeper. But
one does not have to glance down into the gorge. A zigzag
path with good steps. The crosshatchings on the map are
no exaggeration; on the far side of the gorge there are
cliffs and a waterfall dissolving into spray—

A third gully presents no problems.

The house Geiser left at dawn, his house, standing now
in a different valley, seems hardly to belong to the present
any more when Geiser reflects that he has been living there
for fourteen years.

Usually on a walk one thinks of nothing.

The important thing is the next step and the one after that,
so that one does not twist an ankle, one's knees do not give
way, one does not slip suddenly. The umbrella is no use
as a walking stick, it frequently slides on the stones and
offers no support when one's footing is uncertain. But the
path is still good, just now and again the steps in the stones
are too high for someone whose knees have already become
wobbly.

At times Geiser is beginning to think—

Suddenly it is his calves that go on strike; a pain at every
step like being pricked by needles. The Maggia valley may
already be in sight, its green plain spread out below, but
the houses on it still look no bigger than toys, and it is better just to keep his eyes on the path.

77

At one point the path leads uphill again—

A chapel with an overhanging roof, and even a seat under the shelter of the porch, provides a chance to sit down and shake off the cramp in his calves; it is marked on the map, which is always comforting: one knows from a map exactly where one is at a particular moment; in somewhat less than an hour he has descended more than four hundred meters, and now there is not far to go:

Another 313 meters downhill.

The ants in his rucksack do not disturb him; Geiser permits himself a little cognac, then a glance down into the gorge, where almost certainly no human being has ever set foot, and a glance upward: ridges and cracks, slopes so steep that one wonders how one ever descended them. It is a tangled sort of valley.

It is now around two o'clock.

What is there to think about?

—$EB : AE = AE : AB$

—the Bible and the fresco of the Virgin Mary do not prove that God will continue to exist once human beings, who cannot accept the idea of a creation without a creator, have ceased to exist; the Bible was written by human beings.

—the Alps are the result of folding.

—ants live in colonies.

—the arch was invented by the Romans.

—if the Arctic ice were to melt, New York would be under water, as would Europe, except for the Alps.

—many chestnut trees are cankered.

—only human beings can recognize catastrophes, provided they survive them; Nature recognizes no catastrophes.

—man emerged in the Holocene.

It is almost four o'clock when Geiser wakes up. He has heard only the last faint rolls of thunder; obviously there was a brief rainfall. Clouds encircling the steep mountains, but billowy clouds, full of light, almost sunshine. In a little while one may even see blue sky here and there. Drops falling from the trees, which are glistening, and a twittering in the glistening leaves.

The cramp in his calves has subsided.

The church in Aurigeno (from which a mail bus runs to Locarno) is not yet visible, but Geiser can quite distinctly hear its clock striking the hour; a harsh, hoarse bell, with hardly any reverberations.

The ants have disappeared.

After finishing the cognac (a small flask), placing his field glasses in the rucksack, and slowly tying the rucksack up again, Geiser remains seated for a while, not telling himself what he is thinking, what he has decided in his head.

Then he rises, straps the rucksack to his back, looks around to make sure that he has not left an Ovomaltine wrapping on the ground or on the bench in front of the chapel—which is not, incidentally, a chapel. It is just a fresco of the Virgin Mary with an overhanging roof.

Geiser almost forgot his umbrella.

The ascent is laborious, just as he expected, and Geiser knows that it is four hundred meters up to the pass. The confident knowledge that the three gullies are not insuperable, that the track is a good one on the whole and not dangerous so long as there is daylight, and that the zigzag path in front of him is not interminable—these things hearten him, even though a path known only from the descent can often be unrecognizable when one comes to ascend it. It is not his calves that are on strike now, but his thighs. When will he reach the second gully, the large one? There are stretches Geiser cannot remember; all the same, there they are, fairly steep, and now and again, in order to surmount a high step, Geiser has to provide help for his thighs by putting a supporting hand, the right one, on a knee; the left hand is holding the umbrella as a walking stick. With increasing frequency Geiser finds it necessary to sit down on the nearest bank to regain his breath, both hands grasping the handle of his umbrella, his chin resting on his hands.

What use would Basel be to him?

By the time he reaches the pass, it is already about seven in the evening and growing dusky; at the pass it is raining again.

It has been a long day.

Once more the open pasture, where the path disappears, where in the morning Geiser enjoyed the thought that nobody could know where Herr Geiser was at this moment—

Nobody knows it now, either.

—and once more the wide stretch of water without a bridge:

The water over the debris is flowing no more swiftly, but it is now dark, and not even the best flashlight casts much of a beam in the rain. What it principally shows is glittering needles of rain. Each time he felt distrustful of the next stone within stepping distance, Geiser turned back. Here and there a vigorous leap would probably have done it, but Geiser no longer trusted his legs. If nobody was to know about this expedition, it was important to avoid an accident of any kind, even something as simple as a fractured arm. Once he tried still farther up, then lower down. He took his time about it—no one at home, waiting and counting the hours—no giving in to hastiness. Everywhere the same wash of water; with the difference that it is easier in daylight to guess where the water is deep or shallow. The thought that if, on the bench in front of the Virgin Mary, he had not chosen to return, he might now be sitting on a train or in a restaurant, was not exactly helpful when Geiser was standing on a stone surrounded by water as far as the flashlight could reach, and when even to turn back was risky; a stone on which he had previously stepped seemed to have shifted, and water was washing over it. What now? In the end he did lose patience, and closed his umbrella: one needs both arms free to keep one's balance. Suddenly the water was up to his knees, and after he lost his prodding umbrella, it became difficult for him to stand upright in the water—but he made it without losing his flashlight, and a flashlight was more important now than an umbrella.

A path is a path even at night.

As long as one keeps on walking, exhaustion is almost a pleasant feeling in one's veins, and Geiser knows he must not stop now to sit down; otherwise he will find himself unable to get to his feet again.

There is always ground, even at night.

What can be seen in the glimmer of a flashlight is for the most part enough for him: slabs, indicating a path, the next step, then woodland soil with roots, tree trunks on both sides, but a drop either to the left or to the right, then once more slabs in the bracken, debris and thistles, at one point a dead tree root, and beyond it nothing but glittering needles of rain—bottomless night, forcing one to go, not forward, but back, and there is the path again, and the sharp bend Geiser had overlooked before, clear to see. At times Geiser has the feeling that he knows more or less where he is, that he should now be approaching the meadow with the barns. Instead, more woods. Perhaps he did not see the barns he was expecting because they lay beyond the radius of his flashlight. Even when rain is streaming down, one ceases to notice it after a while. For the past two hours Geiser has simply been walking, not even wishing to know where he is. Now and then a knee gives way, but only once has he fallen. Woodland soil and pine needles sticking to his hands, but nothing more. The path is leading downward, and that is the main thing. The barns he has been expecting for the past hour come suddenly into sight. Geiser might have taken shelter there, but what is the point, when he is shivering in wet clothes? It cannot get any darker than it has been so far. What will come next Geiser already knows: a zigzag through the woods, in which one must be careful not to miss a bend, and later on the bridge with its twisted tubular railings; after that the path becomes more even, a good path that cannot be missed, so long as the battery of the flashlight holds out—

Nobody will ever hear about his outing.

Every time Geiser found it necessary to stop for a while and wait until his heart ceased its heavy pounding, he switched off his flashlight to preserve the battery.

What use would Basel be to him?

The village was asleep, it was past midnight when Geiser reached home, unseen by anyone.

In the Ice Age one arm of the Maggia glacier stretched across the Passo della Garina (1,076 meters), leaving only the Salmone peak barely showing above the massive sheet of ice.

The soup, the minestrone that Geiser emptied out into the grounds days ago, is back, a whole basinful, beside it a

83

reprint from a scientific periodical with a greeting, in pencil, from the German professor; obviously during the day, while Geiser was asleep, someone had come to the house, and surely not without ringing the doorbell.

What is the cure for aching limbs?

Whether today it is still raining or raining again, whether the rain is coming down diagonally or vertically, whether it is possible at this moment to see the village and the whole valley, or just the nearest fir tree in the mist, the raindrops gliding slowly down the wires, the glistening, dripping ivy —these are things in which Geiser can take no interest.

The graze on his hand is not worth bothering about.

The spotted salamander in the bathroom—

Once already Geiser meant to fetch the shovel to pitch the slimy monster out into the grounds, but on the way to fetch it, he forgot.

The banisters without a handrail—

Whoever it was who brought the soup, the solar investigator in person or his wife or his daughter, somebody saw the papers on the wall; this is more annoying than the aching limbs (the thighs in particular), and there is now something even more urgent than the shovel for the spotted salamander—that Geiser should lock his front door.

Geiser has no wish to leave the valley.

(He could have done so!)

The solar investigator's essay, a lecture given at an international congress, is fairly comprehensible for a layman using the dictionary of foreign words, until it comes to the mathematical formulas. Geiser skipped the first of these, but unfortunately there are more of them, chemical ones, and Geiser has to give up.

(All the things one has never learned!)

The hot plate is growing warm—

Two statesmen greeting each other in some airport, it is all still going on, and when later one looks again: advertisements for all kinds of things one will never need.

The front door is now locked.

The hot plate is glowing.

When a house catches fire here in the valley, firemen come from the neighboring villages, mostly people getting on in years; by the time they bring the hoses to the right spot and screw them together, the beams beneath the heavy granite tiles of the roof are ablaze, and when shortly afterward the roof collapses, the tiles' weight carries them down through the ceiling and then through the floor, to crash to pieces in the cellar.

The hot plate is turned off.

At the moment Geiser is standing before his gallery of papers.

18 And the Lord God said, It is not good that the man should be alone; I will make him an help meet for him.

19 And out of the ground the Lord God formed every beast of the field, and every fowl of the air; and brought them unto Adam to see what he would call them: and whatsoever Adam called every living creature, that was the name thereof.

20 And Adam gave names to all cattle, and to the fowl of the air, and to every beast of the field; but for Adam there was not found an help meet for him.

PLESIOSAUR
DIPLODOCUS
DIMETRODON
DINOCERAS
ANTRODEMUS
TYRANNOSAURUS
RHAMPHORHYNCHUS
MAMMOTH
CERATODUS
ICHTHYOSAUR
TRICERATOPS
TRINACROMERUM
ARCHAEOPTERYX
STEGOSAUR
RHINOCEROS
PALAEOSCINCUS
DIPLOCAULUS
SYNDYOCERAS
DSUNGARIPTERUS

LEPTOLEPIS
ENDOTHIODON
HESPERORNIS
PTERODACTYL
GLYPTODON
EOHIPPUS
TETRABELODON
PTERICHTHYS
ETC.

The vital functions of human beings and animals are influenced by thunderstorms to the extent that unstable weather conditions (*see* Weather) exacerbate the responses of the sympathetic nervous system. In human beings, circulatory disturbances in the capillaries of the skin have been noted, and, independently of these, a temporary aggravation of certain skin diseases (eczema, prickly heat), while embolisms can occur more frequently on days when the atmosphere is thundery. It is sometimes asserted that attacks of glaucoma, epilepsy, and eclampsia occur more frequently during thunderstorms than at other times, but there is little proof of this. As a general rule it can be stated that, in both human beings and animals, the psychological effects of a thunderstorm (feelings of anxiety or tension) tend to outweigh the physical ones (the occasioning or aggravation of an illness).

Cutting things out with the nail scissors has the advantage of enabling Geiser to make quicker progress; not only that, but the tape also adheres to wall plaster, so that he can now use all the walls; the new method may ruin his books, but it has the further advantage that he can now stick illustrations on the wall.

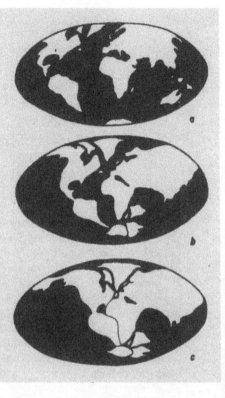

Ill. 68. Wegener's theory of continental drift; the earth today (a), in the Late Cretaceous (b), in the Jurassic (c). Drawing: R. Steel, 1968

Ill. 11. Compsognathus, a Coelurosaur, Solnhofen limestone, Jachenhausen (E. Bavaria), about the size of a cat. After F. v. Huene

88

Ill. 54. **Kentrosaurus aethiopicus,** a stegosaur from East Africa, Late Jurassic, length approx. 5 meters. Drawing: R. Steel, 1968

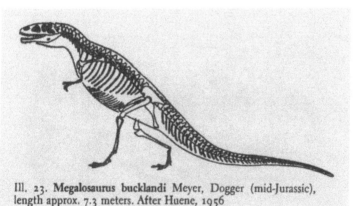

Ill. 23. **Megalosaurus bucklandi** Meyer, Dogger (mid-Jurassic), length approx. 7.3 meters. After Huene, 1956

Something Geiser has not taken into account: that the text on the back of the page might perhaps be no less illuminating than the picture on the front that he has so carefully cut out; now this text has been cut to pieces, useless for his gallery.

Ill. 26. **Tyrannosaurus rex**, one of the largest carnosaurs, length approx. 15 meters. Original drawing: R. Steel, 1968

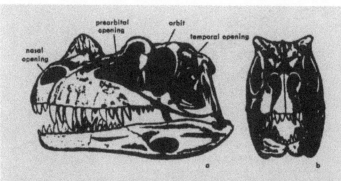

Ill. 24. **Ceratosaurus nasicornis Marsh**, skull, length 63 centimeters, Late Jurassic, Colorado. After O. C. Marsh

Now and again Geiser finds himself wondering what he really wants to know, what he hopes to gain from all this knowledge.

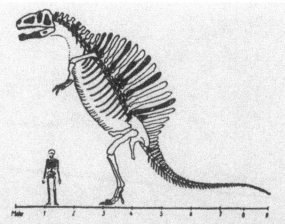

Ill. 27. Spinosaurus, reconstructed skeleton, beside it a human skeleton, Cretaceous, Egypt. After Stromer

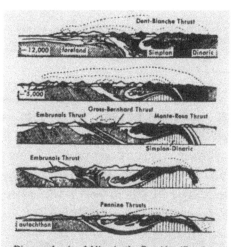

Diagram showing folding in the Pennides (Pennine Alps), based on Argand. The sections west of Simplon show the orological construction to a depth of 12 kilometers: its ramifications are revealed most clearly in the Monte-Rosa Thrust. The uppermost thrust (Dent-Blanche Thrust, to which the Matterhorn belongs) forms the connecting link between the Western Alps (Wallis), Graubünden, and the Eastern Alps (Grossglockner).

91

Ill. 2. Skeleton of the carnosaur **Ornithosuchus**, Trías, length approx. 4 meters (above), and of **Stagonolepis**, a pseudosuchian (Trías), both members of the dinosaurs' ancestral group. After Walker. Krebs (1969) places **Ornithosuchus** among the pseudosuchians on account of its foot structure.

It is clear that Geiser must have been wearing his hat. Otherwise it would not be lying beside him on the floor. It is daytime. Why are all the lights on in the house? The fire is still glowing. Geiser finds he can sit up. No bones broken; at any rate no pains anywhere. He is just feeling dizzy, which is why he has to wait a while before venturing to rise to his feet like a human being.

His spectacles lying on the floor are not broken.

Presumably—he cannot remember—Geiser fell down the stairs, because of the absence of the familiar handrail.

The house is still standing, unharmed.

Since yesterday—Geiser remembers this—the mail bus has been running again. One hears its triadic horn sounding in the valley: first loud, then soft, since the highway passes through a gorge to one side, then, after the next curve, louder than before; for a while the bus's motor can be heard, then it suddenly grows quiet again, the bus having vanished around the curve, and only five minutes later a muffled, triadic hoot from far away—

Geiser can hear that.

There is a mirror in the bathroom in which he might see whether he has a cut on his face. But there is no hurry. The handkerchief he just pressed to his face shows no blood, not a single drop.

The front door is locked.

Actually Geiser is not at the bottom of the stairs, but on the floor beside the table; a chair has fallen over—

The mirror reveals no cut on his face.

The spotted salamander is still in the bathroom.

It is his left eyelid. No pain. When one puts a finger on it, there is no feeling at all in the eyelid. Later, there was a ring at the front door. The power is on again, of course, and Geiser is not deaf. The bell kept on ringing.

Geiser wants no visitors.

In the kitchen there are still: almonds, a jar of pickled

gherkins, honey, onions, a jar of olives, canned tomatoes, flour, semolina, oatmeal in plenty; no need for Geiser to leave the house.

All the same, he has his hat on his head.

It is not unusual for a large log (chestnut) still to be glowing on the following morning. Seven or eight hours could have passed since Geiser had his fall—

Perhaps the chair slipped.

Lying on the table are the twelve volumes of the encyclopedia, as well as the magnifying glass, the nail scissors, and various bits of paper, scraps of print that Geiser had cut out but not yet stuck to the wall.

There is still a lot to be done—

Perhaps it is his daughter who keeps telephoning; she probably tried to get through days ago, when the lines were cut, and now she keeps on trying.

The telephone rings all through the morning.

What is there to tell her:

—debris among the lettuces, but the mail bus is running again, the sunflowers all snapped in the middle, a lot of nuts in the grass, autumn crocuses already out in August . . .

Geiser looks for the tape.

—damage down in the valley . . .

He has found the tape.

Standing before his gallery, Geiser cannot remember what gave him the idea of cutting out illustrations of dinosaurs and lizards and sticking them to the wall—

There were never any dinosaurs in Ticino.

Toward noon the telephone stops ringing.

Probably the solar investigator has departed, since the highway is no longer blocked, and it was the solar investigator who rang the doorbell in the morning, to say goodbye until next year.

—there have been some landslides. . . .

A crack in the plaster, fine as a hair, which was not there yesterday—that could spell trouble, as could a crack in the floor tiles in the kitchen; this could mean, not that the whole slope is about to slide, but that the house might no longer be able to withstand the pressure of the water coming down the slope.

(This once caused the collapse of a church.)

But it is not a crack, only a piece of string that Geiser saw on the kitchen floor. If he ties something heavy to the string, an empty bottle for instance, to ensure that the string remains perpendicular, and if he holds this up against the wall, he will see that the walls and the whole house are still in line.

The eyelid, the left one, is still numb.

Otherwise nothing has happened.

When Geiser looks in the mirror again to see his face, he knows that the name of his daughter in Basel is Corinne, and that the firm in Basel that his son-in-law has been managing, and which has since trebled its output, bears his name, even if Geiser does look like a newt.

The spotted salamander is no longer in the bathroom.

Geiser has thrown it into the fire.

A flameless glow, a noiseless smoldering beneath the ash, and when one puts a dry piece of wood on top, first a blue flicker, then a flame; at first it crackles loudly, then later it glows for a while in silence; when a large log, partly charred, suddenly disintegrates into smoldering fragments, the familiar sound—

Geiser is not deaf.

Geiser knows the year of his birth and the first names of his parents, also his mother's maiden name, and the name of the street in Basel in which he was born, the number of the house—

(The things a newt knows.)

Geiser is not a newt.

It has been raining a lot in Basel, too, the railroad across the Gotthard was blocked for two days, there were floods in upper Italy, and several people lost their lives.

The tight feeling above his left temple persists.

Geiser cannot remember what he said to Corinne, she knew everything from the newspaper anyway; not the faintest idea what he, Geiser, told her.

At some time a stray dog in the grounds—

Since yesterday, when he roasted the cat over the fire and then was unable to eat it, Geiser can no longer face even the soup, because there is bacon in it.

Geiser did not tell her about that.

It is a mongrel that does not belong to the village, nor is it the Dutch people's dog—they have presumably left by now; it is sniffing for scent marks in the grounds, but it finds none.

Kitty is buried near the roses.

It is not raining.

The soup, the minestrone, the sight or smell of which he can no longer bear, Geiser has thrown into the nettles.

The stray dog has gone.

Later, three men came: the parish clerk Francesco, old Ettore, the laborer who has been working all his life on supporting walls and does not believe the whole mountain could ever begin to slide, and another man; they rang and rang at the front door, as if he were deaf, and shouted, and beat their fists against the door, then finally walked around the house and shone flashlights into the downstairs rooms; it was not until Geiser threw a cup at them that they disappeared.

But that was not today.

It was during the night; otherwise they would not have been using their flashlights, and today the sun is shining.

At once the birds start singing again.

Geiser has closed the shutters; it is not right for strangers to gawk through the windows, just because one refuses to open the front door.

Geiser knows what he looks like.

(A newt doesn't even know that.)

Geiser knows, for example, that:

—when climbing a ridge at two in the morning, one needs no lantern, so bright is it above the glaciers, even when no moon is shining; the rock is the color of bone, not gray or black, but pale like a bone, and since there are no shadows, it seems unreal, even from close up; but one cannot deny it is there, icy to the touch, and hard as steel; not solid rock—here and there it crumbles when one tries to get a grip on it, and splinters go scattering downward. Not a sound, except for those one is making oneself; now and again the sharp ring of an ice pick tapping against rock; otherwise it is as still as the moon. The peaks and towers seem a jumbled mass when one glances up at them during the night; but later, in the first rays of the sun and against the blue morning sky, they look like yellow amber, while the Zermatt valley is still lying in shadow—

That was fifty years ago.

His Matterhorn story is well known, Geiser has told it so often that even his grandchildren are tired of it.

What are the names of his three grandchildren?

Two hours out there on the face, making no progress, to left and right steep snow slopes, frozen over, interspersed with slabs of smooth slate and rivulets of melting snow, two whole hours without safeguard for either of them—

That was all a long time ago.

Like the yellow sandstorm outside Baghdad.

The power is on again, there is no tapping on sheet metal, not even sounds of splashing, no thunder, no gurgling around the house—

Klaus is buried in Baghdad.

The climb to the summit was calculated to take eight hours, and although they never moved at the same time or without the orthodox safeguard of a taut rope, they made good progress, paying out their rope length by length. By the time they reached the Solvay hut (4,003 meters above sea level), they had passed two other roped parties, one of them with a guide. It was only after this that they came to a little new snow among the rocks, powdery, easy to brush away with a hand, and when occasionally they had to cross packed snow, Klaus, his brother, stamped out good footholds, or cut them out with his pick. The shape of the Matterhorn is familiar from countless pictures; but from close up, when one is leaning against a rock, granting oneself a short rest, the rope looped around a trustworthy boulder, there is nothing of this shape to be seen as one looks around; just jagged peaks and steep slabs and gigantic rocks, not all of them vertical, either, but overhanging, and one marvels that they have not broken off long since and hurtled down into the valley. At anxious moments, which they were unwilling to admit to each other, it was best to keep silent, to adopt a cool air of unconcern as the other searched for holds or for a crack in the rock in which a shoe could find a reasonably firm place. The weather remained excellent, just light clouds above the summit. In places it was as easy as child's play; one does not have to glance up at the wall above, or look down. Klaus was carrying the rucksack. Suddenly, shortly aften ten o'clock, they found themselves standing beside the iron cross on the summit, proud, yet a little disappointed. So this is it! Standing on the Matterhorn eating a cold apple, while yet another roped party arrives, one they had not overtaken: two men and a Japanese girl. From the summit there was not much to see. Here and there a break in the clouds: a view of bleak moraines or the dirty tongue of a glacier, elsewhere a green Alpine meadow in sunshine, streams like a network of white veins, and once they caught sight of the little lake, the Schwarzsee, beside which their green tent was pitched, though they could not spot it, a small ink-blue pool glistening in the sunshine, next to some things that looked like white maggots, presumably cows—

The names of his grandchildren:

SONJA

(surname: Krättli)

HANSJÖRG

—but what is the little girl called?

On the other hand, Geiser does remember:

The mountain guide whom they had overtaken did not respond to their greeting on the summit, but served his German customers with hot tea, and only a long time later —the wind had meanwhile become so strong that almost all of them, whether drinking tea or not, were facing in the same direction with their hair blown forward, or, in the case of those wearing woolen caps, trousers and jackets blown forward—only later, when Klaus inquired about something, did the guide remark to them that, in overtaking him, they had dislodged some stones, more than once in fact— According to the guide there was nothing to fear from the weather. Now and again blue sky could be seen among the racing clouds. As they began the descent they felt apprehensive, for during a descent one has to look downward all the time, and often all one can see are the nearest rocks, hanging over a void; beneath them, a place for birds. It is a long ridge, as they now knew. Klaus this time the end man: he made things safe by throwing the rope around a projection on the rock, so nothing much could happen to the man in front, even if he were to slip. For Klaus himself it was more difficult. Since, as end man, he could not always safeguard himself, their progress could not be measured in rope lengths. The descent was slower than the ascent. It is impossible to keep to the ridge throughout; here there is a spur of rock (a *gendarme*) to get past, there a steep furrow (*couloir*) leading to the right or left of the rock face, so that one regains the ridge only lower down. It was the east face: suddenly they found themselves standing, without any safeguard at all, some seven hundred meters above the bergschrund. No idea how they came to be on this ledge; beside them the steep snow slopes, frozen over, interspersed with slabs of smooth slate and rivulets of melting snow. It was midday. To retrace their steps proved impossible. Once they heard a roped party on the ridge nearby, though they could not see it, just hear voices and the ringing tone of a pick striking against rock. They did not call for help. An hour passed, and shadows began to creep across the face, though the ridge, whose projections they could see below them, was still in the sun. Later, when they started to shout, making funnels out of their hands, there was no one on the ridge—at any rate, not at this height. They had no climbing irons with them, no *piton* that would have enabled them to descend by rope to a strip of packed snow leading to the ridge. Both had fairly adequate footholds, but hardly anything for a handhold. It was as if the face were pushing one outward. But at least there were no falling stones, so long as they kept still. It had been a mistake to venture out on the face at this point, in order to avoid a tortuous climb along the ridge; all the other roped parties had kept to the ridge. What they did then, when they knew they were alone, was madness: in order to reach the strip of packed snow below, Klaus had to make do with tiny cracks in the rock; the rope, which his brother wound around his shoulders and paid out slowly, could never have held him up—they would both have fallen. And they knew it. It was a matter of only ten or twelve meters, but it lasted forever. And the question still remained whether they would be able to move on from the strip of packed snow. Twice Klaus, with both hands in a crack, had to stretch his entire length downward, feeling for a foothold; it was now impossible to turn back; nobody could pull himself upward from that position. The strip of packed snow, narrow but not too steep, was their last hope of getting off the face. Since neither could do anything to safeguard the other, it was of course senseless to remain roped together. The packed snow on the narrow strip was obviously too thin for Klaus to anchor the ice pick, in order to secure himself after a fashion with a loop of the rope; it was, however, still fairly soft, though the sun had been off it for half an hour; it was possible to stamp it. Klaus had given instructions that, as soon as he reached firm rock again and had a reliable foothold, his younger brother should take off the rope, so that Klaus could continue climbing. The final meters he had to negotiate solely by dangling both feet without hold. Then Klaus gave the signal. The rope fell in a curve, the end he had released twining far below, but Klaus managed to keep a grip on his end. Slowly he pulled the long rope back and looped it around his shoulders. Then he vanished from sight. His intention was to try to reach the ridge by himself, since he was the elder, and then to climb back up the ridge and lower the rope, properly secured, from above. If this did not work, Klaus said, he would make the descent by himself and fetch help, which would arrive probably sometime around midnight. Such had been the arrangement. But to stand there alone against the face, both shoes wedged in a crack, unable to move, looking down on the glacier—nobody could have held out till midnight. Even half an hour would have been too long. In the meantime it had turned cold; no wind, but the sort of cold that leads to indifference. No means of keeping in touch. Whether his brother was still trying to lower the rope from above, or whether, this attempt having failed for some reason, he was now on his way down, it was impossible to know. Once some fragments of slate came sliding down the wall; but no rope.

That remains in his memory.

Klaus was a good brother.

And Corinne is an affectionate daughter—

What she wants to know has nothing to do with the Matterhorn, that was fifty years ago, and Corinne is here to find out what is going on now.

There have been some landslides.

But the highway is open again—

Otherwise Corinne would not be here.

At last the rope came sliding slowly over the rock, one arm's length after another; but it was not long enough. Fortunately they had arranged it all; exactly five minutes later, Klaus hauled the empty rope up again, one arm's length after another, and packed snow came clattering down, fragments of ice, two or three stones hurtled by, bounced on the rock farther down, and vanished silently in a wide arc into the void. A quarter of an hour later the rope came down again, this time long enough, but it dangled two or three meters from the face and was difficult to get hold of; he succeeded at last with the help of his ice pick—

All that was a long time ago.

What Corinne wants to know: why the closed shutters, why all these papers on the wall, why his hat on his head?

This is today.

Obviously the men went away, they did not break the front door down, it was not necessary, since Corinne has a key.

Why does she talk to him as if he were a child?

There would still be many things to stick to the wall if there were any point in it; the Magic Tape is useless; a puff of air as Corinne opens the shutters and the slips of paper are lying on the floor, a confused heap that makes no sense.

There is no sugar left.

Corinne does not even take off her coat before she starts making tea. His son-in-law in Basel, who always knows best, sends his regards.

There will never be a pagoda—

Geiser knows that.

But there is still some crispbread left.

A dry-stone wall has collapsed, debris among the lettuces, and the highway was blocked, but Corinne has heard that already.

There is nothing to say.

His eyelid is numb, the corner of his mouth, too; Geiser knows it, and a hat on one's head is no help for that.

Today the sun is shining.

What to do with all these bits of paper?

When Corinne brings in the tea, her eyes are moist, though she does not seem aware of it; she smiles like a hospital nurse and talks to her father as if he were a child.

The banisters without a handrail—

The books with their pages snipped—

The ants Geiser recently observed under a dripping fir tree are not concerned with what anyone might know about them; nor were the dinosaurs, which died out before a human being set eyes on them. All the papers, whether on the wall or on the carpet, can go. Who cares about the Holocene? Nature needs no names. Geiser knows that. The rocks do not need his memory.

Erosion (Lat. *erodere* = to gnaw), in the broad sense the processes (water, wind, ice) by which the surface of the earth is worn away; in a narrower sense the gouging and denuding action of flowing water. The extent of erosion is dependent on the strength of the flow, the resistance of the stone, and the nature of the ground. Through deepening and widening the original river bed, it leads to the formation of valleys. Geological erosion, or abrasion, is, in its natural occurrence, a beneficial process, though human interference and mismanagement can lead to catastrophes, caused by disturbing the natural balance (e.g., the "dust bowl" in the western U.S.A.). Such catastrophes are brought about by the destruction of natural vegetation and overcultivation of the soil, etc.

The chestnut, a native of Asia Minor, was originally brought to Greece around 500 B.C., and to Italy slightly later. The chestnut trees at the foot of the Alps were first planted by the Romans. These trees reach a height of 20–30 meters and flourish for a period of 70–140 years. After this they usually become hollow.

Eschatology (f. Gr. *éskhatos* = last), theology of "the last things," i.e., the final fate of the individual human being and of the world.

Coherent (Lat.): remaining together, consistent. Coherence: the quality of remaining together; in *optics*, used to describe bundles of light having the same wavelengths and vibrations. Coherence factor: *psych.*, single impressions forming a configuration through spatial proximity, similarity, symmetry, etc. Principle of coherence: *phil.*, principle of the connection between all existing things.

Chestnut canker was first discovered in 1904 in the vicinity of New York. Six years after its initial appearance 2% of the trees had died; after 8 years the proportion rose to 95%. The disease spread to Italy after the war. In the year 1948 a similar disease appeared for the first time in Ticino (Monte Ceneri). The disease, which kills off the trees, is caused by a fungus that scientists call "endothia parasitica." A remedy is still being sought, but the epidemic, which is spreading as inexorably as the Black Death of the Middle Ages, is difficult to treat. Are we facing the destruction of all the chestnut woods in Ticino?

At the time of their supremacy the Romans established military colonies in these districts, too. To judge from the Roman remains discovered there, the colony at Locarno must have been one of great importance. Evidence suggests that it was settled by experienced soldiers, cohorts whose active campaigning lay behind them.

Apoplexy, known popularly as a stroke, is a sudden loss of brain function, combined usually with paralysis and loss of consciousness, and often accompanied by loss of speech (*aphasia*). The usual cause is the bursting of a cerebral blood vessel due to arteriosclerosis or hypertension, and the extent of the hemorrhage may be slight, or located in parts of the brain where its presence gives rise to little disturbance. Unless the vital areas at the base of the brain have been affected, in which case death is likely to occur within a short period, a fair measure of recovery is possible. Another cause of the loss of brain function is the blocking of a cerebral blood vessel, preventing blood from reaching the brain (*embolism*). The paralysis usually affects only one side of the body (*hemiplegia*); when the hemorrhage is in the left part of the brain, the right side of the body is affected, and vice versa. The paralyzed limbs are at first slack and immobile, but eventually they pass into a spastic stage.

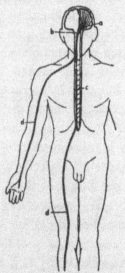

Apoplexy: diagram showing an apoplectic stroke in the

109

The village stands unharmed. Above the mountains, high up in the blue sky, the white trails of passenger planes that cannot be heard. The scent of lavender, bees, during the day it becomes almost hot, summer as usual. The walls in the sun are swarming with lizards, they lie basking on the stone window sills or flit silently up and down the walls of the house. They will never grow larger than lizards. Now and again one hears the sound of a power saw, the shrill whine as the saw eats into a tree trunk, and a little later, after one has heard a sudden rustling somewhere in the undergrowth and the dull thud of a felled tree, the crackle of its idling. Many chestnut trees are cankered. Figs do not ripen, but grapes do. When they are ripe, the chestnuts fall to the ground with a noise that makes one jump. All in all, a quiet valley. Now and again one hears a helicopter and even sees it for a while; a bundle of roof beams swaying on a wire cable, here and there in the valley construction work is still going on. For half a minute its noise flickers over the village, drowning all voices; but once it has disappeared behind the woods there is peace again. As in the Middle Ages. Minutes later it comes flickering back, this time in a narrower curve, and fetches its next load, a ton of cement. Apart from that, little happens. Twice a week the blonde butcher woman drives the length of the valley, selling meat and sausages from her Volkswagen. All in all, no deserted valley; there are butterflies, there are vipers, though one seldom sees them, and, where people live, there are chickens. The church clock strikes each hour twice, in case one has neglected to count properly. In October the first snow may suddenly appear on the mountaintops; if the sun is shining, it melts within two or three days. The glaciers, which once stretched as far as Milan, are retreating. There are ravines that the sun never reaches in the winter; there one sees icicles like organ pipes. In the places the sun does reach one can often go walking in the winter without a coat, unless it is snowing, so warm is it at midday, though the earth remains frozen. In the spring there are camellias, and in the summer one sees tents here and there, people swimming in the cold stream or lying on the sunny rocks. State and canton do everything to ensure that the valley does not die; mail bus thrice daily. Panning for gold in the streams has never been worth the trouble. All in all, a green valley, wooded as in the Stone Age. There are no plans for a reservoir. In August and September, at night, there are shooting stars to be seen, or one hears the call of a little owl.

Pages 10–11: Giulio Rossi and Eligio Pometta, *Geschichte des Kantons Tessin*, Bern, 1944.

Pages 13–14, 50: Giovanni Anastasi, *Tessiner Leben*, Zürich.

Pages 16–17: Piero Bianconi, *Locarno*, Zürich, 1972.

Pages 17, 109: J. Hardmeyer, *Locarno und seine Täler*, Zürich, 1923.

Pages 17–18: *Der Lago Maggiore und seine Täler*, Leipzig, 1910.

Pages 18, 28, 35–37, 39, 53–54, 61, 62, 65, 68–69, 87, 91, 109: *Der Grosse Brockhaus*, in twelve volumes, 16th, fully revised edition, Wiesbaden, 1953.

Pages 43, 50, 83, 108: *Locarno*, Schweizer Wanderbuch 23, Bern, 1969.

Pages 61–62: *Schweizer Lexikon in zwei Bänden*, Zürich, 1949.

Pages 63–64: *Die Welt in der wir leben*, Zürich, 1956.

Pages 88–92: Rodney Steel, "Die Dinosaurier," Wittenberg Lutherstadt, 1970.

Pages 107, 108: *Der Grosse Duden*, Volume 5, Fremdwörterbuch (Dictionary of Foreign Words), Mannheim, 1974.

Page 108: Konrad Bächinger, *Tessin*, Arbeitshefte für den Unterricht in Schweizer Geografie (Workbook for the Study of Swiss Geography), St. Gallen, 1970.

SELECTED DALKEY ARCHIVE PAPERBACKS

PETROS ABATZOGLOU, *What Does Mrs. Freeman Want?*
PIERRE ALBERT-BIROT, *Grabinoulor.*
YUZ ALESHKOVSKY, *Kangaroo.*
FELIPE ALFAU, *Chromos.*
   Locos.
IVAN ÂNGELO, *The Celebration.*
   The Tower of Glass.
DAVID ANTIN, *Talking.*
DJUNA BARNES, *Ladies Almanack.*
   Ryder.
JOHN BARTH, *LETTERS.*
   Sabbatical.
DONALD BARTHELME, *The King.*
   Paradise.
SVETISLAV BASARA, *Chinese Letter.*
MARK BINELLI, *Sacco and Vanzetti Must Die!*
ANDREI BITOV, *Pushkin House.*
LOUIS PAUL BOON, *Chapel Road.*
   Summer in Termuren.
ROGER BOYLAN, *Killoyle.*
IGNÁCIO DE LOYOLA BRANDÃO, *Teeth under the Sun.*
   Zero.
CHRISTINE BROOKE-ROSE, *Amalgamemnon.*
BRIGID BROPHY, *In Transit.*
MEREDITH BROSNAN, *Mr. Dynamite.*
GERALD L. BRUNS,
   Modern Poetry and the Idea of Language.
GABRIELLE BURTON, *Heartbreak Hotel.*
MICHEL BUTOR, *Degrees.*
   Mobile.
   Portrait of the Artist as a Young Ape.
G. CABRERA INFANTE, *Infante's Inferno.*
   Three Trapped Tigers.
JULIETA CAMPOS, *The Fear of Losing Eurydice.*
ANNE CARSON, *Eros the Bittersweet.*
CAMILO JOSÉ CELA, *The Family of Pascual Duarte.*
   The Hive.
   Christ versus Arizona.
LOUIS-FERDINAND CÉLINE, *Castle to Castle.*
   Conversations with Professor Y.
   London Bridge.
   North.
   Rigadoon.
HUGO CHARTERIS, *The Tide Is Right.*
JEROME CHARYN, *The Tar Baby.*
MARC CHOLODENKO, *Mordechai Schamz.*
EMILY HOLMES COLEMAN, *The Shutter of Snow.*
ROBERT COOVER, *A Night at the Movies.*
STANLEY CRAWFORD, *Some Instructions to My Wife.*
ROBERT CREELEY, *Collected Prose.*
RENÉ CREVEL, *Putting My Foot in It.*
RALPH CUSACK, *Cadenza.*
SUSAN DAITCH, *L.C.*
   Storytown.
NIGEL DENNIS, *Cards of Identity.*
PETER DIMOCK,
   A Short Rhetoric for Leaving the Family.
ARIEL DORFMAN, *Konfidenz.*
COLEMAN DOWELL, *The Houses of Children.*
   Island People.
   Too Much Flesh and Jabez.
RIKKI DUCORNET, *The Complete Butcher's Tales.*
   The Fountains of Neptune.
   The Jade Cabinet.
   Phosphor in Dreamland.
   The Stain.
   The Word "Desire."
WILLIAM EASTLAKE, *The Bamboo Bed.*
   Castle Keep.
   Lyric of the Circle Heart.
JEAN ECHENOZ, *Chopin's Move.*
STANLEY ELKIN, *A Bad Man.*
   Boswell: A Modern Comedy.
   Criers and Kibitzers, Kibitzers and Criers.
   The Dick Gibson Show.
   The Franchiser.
   George Mills.
   The Living End.
   The MacGuffin.
   The Magic Kingdom.
   Mrs. Ted Bliss.
   The Rabbi of Lud.
   Van Gogh's Room at Arles.

ANNIE ERNAUX, *Cleaned Out.*
LAUREN FAIRBANKS, *Muzzle Thyself.*
   Sister Carrie.
LESLIE A. FIEDLER,
   Love and Death in the American Novel.
GUSTAVE FLAUBERT, *Bouvard and Pécuchet.*
FORD MADOX FORD, *The March of Literature.*
JON FOSSE, *Melancholy.*
MAX FRISCH, *I'm Not Stiller.*
   Man in the Holocene.
CARLOS FUENTES, *Christopher Unborn.*
   Distant Relations.
   Terra Nostra.
   Where the Air Is Clear.
JANICE GALLOWAY, *Foreign Parts.*
   The Trick Is to Keep Breathing.
WILLIAM H. GASS, *The Tunnel.*
   Willie Masters' Lonesome Wife.
ETIENNE GILSON, *The Arts of the Beautiful.*
   Forms and Substances in the Arts.
C. S. GISCOMBE, *Giscome Road.*
   Here.
DOUGLAS GLOVER, *Bad News of the Heart.*
   The Enamoured Knight.
KAREN ELIZABETH GORDON, *The Red Shoes.*
GEORGI GOSPODINOV, *Natural Novel.*
JUAN GOYTISOLO, *Marks of Identity.*
PATRICK GRAINVILLE, *The Cave of Heaven.*
HENRY GREEN, *Blindness.*
   Concluding.
   Doting.
   Nothing.
JIŘÍ GRUŠA, *The Questionnaire.*
JOHN HAWKES, *Whistlejacket.*
AIDAN HIGGINS, *A Bestiary.*
   Bornholm Night-Ferry.
   Flotsam and Jetsam.
   Langrishe, Go Down.
   Scenes from a Receding Past.
   Windy Arbours.
ALDOUS HUXLEY, *Antic Hay.*
   Crome Yellow.
   Point Counter Point.
   Those Barren Leaves.
   Time Must Have a Stop.
MIKHAIL IOSSEL AND JEFF PARKER, EDS., *Amerika:*
   Contemporary Russians View
   the United States.
GERT JONKE, *Geometric Regional Novel.*
JACQUES JOUET, *Mountain R.*
HUGH KENNER, *The Counterfeiters.*
   Flaubert, Joyce and Beckett:
   The Stoic Comedians.
   Joyce's Voices.
DANILO KIŠ, *Garden, Ashes.*
   A Tomb for Boris Davidovich.
ANITA KONKKA, *A Fool's Paradise.*
GEORGE KONRÁD, *The City Builder.*
TADEUSZ KONWICKI, *A Minor Apocalypse.*
   The Polish Complex.
MENIS KOUMANDAREAS, *Koula.*
ELAINE KRAF, *The Princess of 72nd Street.*
JIM KRUSOE, *Iceland.*
EWA KURYLUK, *Century 21.*
VIOLETTE LEDUC, *La Bâtarde.*
DEBORAH LEVY, *Billy and Girl.*
   Pillow Talk in Europe and Other Places.
JOSÉ LEZAMA LIMA, *Paradiso.*
ROSA LIKSOM, *Dark Paradise.*
OSMAN LINS, *Avalovara.*
   The Queen of the Prisons of Greece.
ALF MAC LOCHLAINN, *The Corpus in the Library.*
   Out of Focus.
RON LOEWINSOHN, *Magnetic Field(s).*
D. KEITH MANO, *Take Five.*
BEN MARCUS, *The Age of Wire and String.*
WALLACE MARKFIELD, *Teitlebaum's Window.*
   To an Early Grave.
DAVID MARKSON, *Reader's Block.*
   Springer's Progress.
   Wittgenstein's Mistress.
CAROLE MASO, *AVA.*

FOR A FULL LIST OF PUBLICATIONS, VISIT:
w w w . d a l k e y a r c h i v e . c o m

SELECTED DALKEY ARCHIVE PAPERBACKS